Love, Pain, and the Whole Damn Thing

Translated from the German by
John E. Woods

ALFRED A. KNOPF    NEW YORK    1989

# Love, Pain, and the Whole Damn Thing

## four stories by Doris Dörrie

THIS IS A BORZOI BOOK
PUBLISHED BY ALFRED A. KNOPF, INC.

Copyright © 1989 by Alfred A. Knopf, Inc.

All rights reserved under International and Pan-American Copyright
Conventions. Published in the United States by Alfred A. Knopf, Inc.,
New York, and simultaneously in Canada by Random House of Canada
Limited, Toronto. Distributed by Random House, Inc., New York.

Originally published in German as *Liebe Schmerz und das ganze
verdammte Zeug* by Diogenes Verlag AG, Zürich, in 1987.
Copyright © 1987 by Diogenes Verlag AG, Zürich

Library of Congress Cataloging-in-Publication Data

Dörrie, Doris [date]
Love, pain and the whole damn thing.

I. Title.
PT2664.073L513    1989    833'.914    88-45772

ISBN 0-394-57799-X

Manufactured in the United States of America
First American Edition

# Contents

Love, Pain, and the Whole Damn Thing

# Straight
# to the
# Heart

After Armin's death, Anna immediately gave away or sold all her electric appliances and had the outlets removed. Except for a few lamps dangling from the ceiling, there was no current flowing anywhere in the house, and as much as Anna sometimes missed her television, her tape recorder, her record player or just a hair dryer, all the same, she preferred doing without the feeling of voltage encircling her and having to tremble for Jan's safety. She simply no longer trusted herself to deal with electricity; she almost feared its revenge . . . but that was silly.

One day, Jan, age four, got a light shock as he touched Anna's shaggy sweater. There was a little spark, and Jan broke into tears. Anna took him in her arms, carried him to her room and laid him on her bed. Jan sobbed loudly, trembling and clinging tightly to her, and Anna knew that he wasn't putting this on, that he had good reason to be panicked. She could feel Armin and the past right behind her and she turned around, brave and defiant, walked to the wardrobe and pulled out the shoe box full of old photographs.

Jan's sobbing ceased. He loved pictures more than anything, grabbing at once for his favorite shot and regarding it carefully, as if he wanted to check whether everything was the same as always: Anna with her shiny saxophone after her first concert. Just turned sixteen, with damp black hair, ugly, happy. Behind her, the drummer. She couldn't even remember his name at the moment. He had been very gentle, and had had a little tuft of very long, black hair on his belly. Like grass. Anna smiled to herself, and though he didn't understand, Jan grinned back at her, his tears forgotten. He rummaged in the box. Anna and Thomas in a fishing boat in Greece. They were gazing indolently in opposite directions. A foolish fellow with exaggerated movements, who told her every day of the six months they spent together that he loved her more than anything. Anna took the snapshot from Jan's hand. Armin in front of the little red Fiat he had given her for her twenty-first birthday and that she was still driving.

. . .

"Was Papa real strong?"

"No, sweetheart—he wasn't strong. But very nice."

"How was he nice?"

"Well, he was very kind to me."

"Were you lovers?" Jan giggled excitedly.

"No," Anna said softly, "we weren't lovers."

Jan shrugged and mixed the photograph back in with the others. She and Angelika, her mother, in her student pad in Munich. Anna had held the camera out at arm's length, put an arm around her mother and pressed the button. All you could see was just half her face, and that half revealed nothing of the expression the face had worn. Farewell snapshot. She hadn't wanted to leave home at all. Angelika was smiling at the camera. Had my mother had enough of me after nineteen years? Angelika's disappointment when Anna failed the entrance exam for the Academy of Music. But no matter what, study she must. Which meant in Munich, so far away from home. She hated the nearby mountains. The room was tiny and expensive and just beneath the roof. Weeds in the gutter at the window. Water stains on the ceiling. Dark in the daytime, quite cozy by night. The gas heater was too big for the little room and you couldn't regulate it. Every fifteen minutes, Anna had to turn it off and open the window. *The American Forces Network* on the radio. Gibberish to fill the silence.

University life was disappointing, not much different from her old high-school life. Her fellow students bored her with their earnestness. In the evening, she would go to the movies alone, or to a bar. That crazy American who was standing next to the entrance, beer mug in hand, grinning to himself. She knew right away that he was an American, because he was wearing heavy hiking-boots and a blue down vest. "You hungry?" she had asked him. "I'm headed home and am going to make myself some spaghetti." That was dumb—but he really was hungry. Without a word but in a good mood, they crossed Leopoldstrasse. He was thirty-five at least, had long gray hair.

On her little hot plate, she made buttered spaghetti, which he praised. He liked Randy Newman, too. As they lay in bed in the dark, her head on his shoulder, Anna grinned: She had just gone out and got herself a "pickup"; he was nice—and had fallen asleep before she could get out of her clothes.

She only saw him once after that. She'd been heading for a lecture one morning and almost stumbled over him on the fourth-floor landing. He was sleeping it off;

hadn't made it to the sixth floor. Anna cut her lecture and fried him some eggs.

He was in love with a German model and, while he waited for her to pay some attention to him, he was reading everything Henry Miller ever wrote.

"Mama, why's your hair blue in this picture with Papa?"

"Oh, Jan. Let Mama just close her eyes for five minutes, won't you? I've got a little headache."

Jan gave her forehead a pat with his warm little hand. Anna smiled, her eyes closed.

Writing papers for her seminars in those days had been pure torture. For hours on end she had crouched there in her room in front of a pile of books. She wasn't interested. She sipped away at Cinzano until her thoughts tangled. Sleep. Often until late into the evening. Bright, pleasant dreams, nothing thrilling, but reason enough to keep her from waking up. She lay there, eyes closed, and waited to glide off to sleep again.

"Make a schedule for each new day," her mother's advice. How humiliating the way humankind white-washed the meaninglessness with a precise daily schedule.

. . .

Her old Latin teacher always said: "Anna, you're a harum-scarum." She couldn't get a handle on the city, got lost in the old town, boarded the wrong streetcars and buses. Those resolute faces all around her made her giddy and clumsy. She stepped on other people's toes, once even lost her footing and landed on top of a seated passenger. Terrified, she got off the bus at once. As if her organs of balance were defective. Too much sleep. Like some sickness but with no pain. Or was she simply downright lethargic? Not a pleasant thought.

She only rarely made decisions, and when she did, they came to her overnight from somewhere far away. One morning she woke up, her head clear and un-fuddled, and knew right away: Today I'm going to dye my hair blue.

It did her good to see how impressed even the trendy British hairdressers on Elisabethstrasse were, how they hemmed and hawed. She waited her turn, a smile on her face, and with gentle disdain thumbed through a women's magazine. Then, while the stinky chemicals did their work in her hair and she still couldn't tell yet just how blue it would turn, Anna relished the hot, exciting feeling of gentle electricity in her body, a feeling she loved so much, but that happened only on rare occasions. The dryer was turned off and swung to one side. Ultramarine blue. Anna glowed. Like some cheap nylon sweater from the rummage box in a discount store.

It didn't bother her that everyone stared, whispered, on the street and in the lecture halls. She had always felt she was different from most people, not better, just different; and her blue hair turned a feeling already present in her mind into a regular picture: a black-and-white photograph with a single splotch of color —Anna Blume. A solitary life, she had vaguely felt it coming on for a long time. She found it horribly taxing to carry on longer conversations. She almost grew dizzy from the boredom, even though she enjoyed talking, but was just never sure whether the way she used words corresponded to customary forms. She wasn't necessarily concerned about being understood. But unlike the state of sleep, being awake left her with the sense of missing something she couldn't give a name to.

During the last sunny days of autumn, she took her saxophone along to the Englischer Garten. The way the sound carried delighted her. A man in his mid-thirties, wearing a heavy, expensive coat that gave him a real squarish shape, stopped and listened for a long time. She could remember very clearly that she had unconsciously taken a step backward to increase the distance between her and this man. She hadn't been playing for money, but the man took his newspaper, spread it out in front of her and on it laid a twenty-mark bill that he weighted down with a small stone. His broad face was flushed. Very earnest bright eyes. Anna watched him while she played. He didn't take his eyes off her, and the way he stood there gazing calmly at her made Anna uneasy. She turned away. Why didn't he move on? Her palms broke into a cold sweat. When she looked back, he was gone, and she could play better again.

Gladioluses. What kitsch. And a whole dozen to boot. They were lying at her door when she came back from the toilet late that night. And a white card in a pompous hand: "I'd like very much to invite you to join me for dinner at the Wolke restaurant, tomorrow evening, 8:30." No signature. The square man. She was sure of it. Annoyed, Anna tossed the card in the wastebasket, but knew at the same time that of course she'd go. Maybe it was that electric feeling and the certainty of knowing for one whole day what she was going to do.

Until six that evening, she stayed in bed. Showered. Washed her hair. The heating coils of her old hair dryer suddenly started glowing dangerously orange, there was a little crackle, and Anna dropped the dryer in fright. Twenty minutes of rubbing her hair dry with a towel. White shadow and black kohl for her eyes. Jeans. No big fuss.

The place was small, elegant and bathed in pleasant yellow light. The waiter led her at once to a table, pulled back the chair and stood behind her until Anna was seated. "Herr Dr. Thal called. He'll be here shortly." Of course. Lawyer or doctor. Her armpits itched from the perfume. Get up and leave, right now.

He was wearing his heavy coat again. "I'm glad," he gave Anna a firm hand. Raindrops glistened on his face. Under the coat, a pastel-blue cashmere sweater. Almost childlike. Armin Thal, dentist. Anna nodded. For her, the pâté and the lobster, please. He ordered the wine. While she drank her aperitif, he gazed at her with that same calm, fixed stare. Anna gave herself a point for holding up under his gaze, counting slowly each time to five, two points if she made it to ten, and three for fifteen. If she evaded his eyes before reaching five, she subtracted a point.

Had scored three points before he began, after a long pause: "Anna, since I saw you yesterday in the Englischer Garten, I've been drawn very strongly to the look you have about you. I've seen how you live because I followed you." The waiter brought the appetizers, and while he set them down, Armin Thal continued calmly: "I have a proposition for you. I live in the country, in a very roomy remodeled farmhouse. You could move in right away, would have two rooms all to yourself and fifteen hundred marks a month. With no strings." She had not been all that surprised. "Let's assume I didn't have blue hair and you had first met me as just a normal student and not as a saxophone player—would you still be making me this offer?" He only flashed a brief smile with his eyes. "You think I'm a very shallow person. No, with or without the blue hair— I'd like to have you around, because in your presence I sense an excitement that unfortunately has been missing in my life for the most part until now." She understood at once. "What sort of excitement is that?" She smiled because her blood suddenly began to course faster. "The excitement of just for once becoming a different person than you already are— because of a second person." Now he was grinning. "An illusion. But so much more intriguing than reality."

"But what happens after a few days or even a few weeks, when the excitement is over . . . then I can leave again, right?"

"No. You would be taking relatively little risk. First

off, I'm thinking of drawing up a contract for a full year, fifteen hundred marks a month."

Anna sucked at the meat in the lobster claws, washed her fingers in a little ceramic bowl of tepid lemon-water.

"Two thousand marks," she said. A long look. Three points.

He folded his hands and laid them before him on the table. Short, round fingers with very small nails.

"Agreed."

Anna drank a sip of wine.

"Maybe."

Her face got a little out of control. Difficulty breathing over espresso and cognac.

She made it to the toilet on her feet. Loud retching, felt better after that. She washed her face, rinsed her mouth and sat down on the cold stone floor. Suddenly exhausted. Makeup smeared.

He quickly paid with a credit card and led her to his car. Anna had trouble focusing her eyes. Without her asking he drove her to her apartment. Climbing the stairs she began to stagger and he supported her arm and bore her quickly and safely to the sixth floor. As he pulled off her jeans she tried to decide whether she found this unpleasant, yet could discover no unambiguous sensation. The safe bed. Even with her eyes closed, she noticed how after a few minutes the lights went out.

She woke up because she felt sick again. Groped for the light switch, but he was already beside her and led her to the washbasin. Bitter gall. He held her and pounded lightly on her back. A doctor. Just forming a thought was too much of an effort now. Around seven o'clock he woke her with tea and zwieback. He was driving to his office now, he said. He laid his telephone number on the nightstand. A fleeting, cool draft crossed her brow as he opened the door and left.

Two hours later Anna had a high fever that put her into a pleasant, gentle trance. She relished her own hot languor, her eyes fixed on the immutable dirty white ceiling with its big brown-rimmed water stain. When Armin came to check on her, she dropped off effortlessly into a deep sleep. He let her be, aired the room and made hot tea for the thermos. After two days she could recognize his footsteps on the stairs.

After four days she knew what she wanted, and the fever broke. Armin showed his delight with a curt nod of the head. They both packed her things. Fun

—and the sense that she had grown years older in a few days. He carried the saxophone down the stairs.

But all the same, as they drove through the city, she somehow felt depressed and intimidated, as if she'd been kidnapped. She opened the window and stuck her head out. The cold wind snapped at her eyes and made her scalp shrink taut. I want to be wild—and there's no holding back if you're wild. She let out a long, high scream that flailed behind the speeding car like a tail.

Armin was content. When they stopped for lights, he stroked the wheel softly with his leather-gloved hands.

The farmhouse surprised her. It was decorated with style, nothing ostentatious. A few pieces of furniture. Big, beautiful carpets. No dog, thank heaven. From her upstairs room she could look out onto endless meadows.

That evening they sat together watching *Only Angels Have Wings* on the VCR. Jean Arthur knew exactly what she wanted, too. Who knows what he wants, never commits himself. The wine was good. They didn't talk much. At twelve-thirty Anna got up. On a whim she gave Armin a kiss on his forehead, which he met with nonchalant, amiable acceptance.

. . .

In bed, she cried a little. Just because—because she didn't know what she ought to be feeling. He woke her at seven with rose tea and two small round buns. Did she want to come along into town? Much too early. Anna declined. Two thousand marks and the contract under her breakfast plate.

Later, curious and with her heart pounding softly, she wandered through the house. In his bedroom, a second VCR. English detective stories. Very few clues about Armin Thal's character. No photographs, no letters. Silk pajamas. In the cellar, just bottles of wine and old furniture.

She read a detective story, watched two movies: *The Red Circle* and *Breathless*. Called her mother. As expected, she was horrified by the move.

Armin brought home steaks and salad fixings that evening. He put on a rock-and-roll record and began washing the lettuce. Amazed that Anna couldn't jitterbug. Jerry Lee Lewis—never heard of him. Born in 1957—how was she supposed to know who he was? Ah yes, Armin laughed softly. He laid the steaks in the skillet.

. . .

After dinner: "Can you play chess?" No, not that, either. He patiently explained it to her. Fire in the fireplace. After two hours she couldn't concentrate anymore. She was sweating, silent. He gazed calmly at her. She got up and paced the room. Upset stomach.

Impatient, she sat down next to him on the arm of his chair and laid an arm around his neck. He gave her a friendly look, but didn't move. Her blue head on his chest. Pleasant. Could it really be he wanted nothing else from her? Impossible. And, yes, at last, he did start caressing her. His skin was firm, smooth and cool. No water stains on the ceiling in his bedroom. Excited and yet nonchalant at the same time, she had felt very free. He was elegant, gentle, used to this, good.

She didn't wake till noon, alone. A long, hot bath. And what difference did it make? No love, no problems. She laughed, and in the large tiled bathroom it sounded louder than she had intended.

She didn't make it to her lecture at three, because the bus into town took over an hour. So instead, she rode to the market and bought fresh fish and vege-

tables. Chocolate pudding for dessert. Armin was en-
chanted. Sole—his favorite. Anna flushed with joy.

She got used to waiting for him. She cooked often,
having discovered what fun it was. They never set a
definite time. Anna was always there.

She didn't register for the summer semester. During
the day, she would sit in the cozy leather armchair
and read or watch movies. Every day had its plan
now: Armin left the house at seven-thirty and returned
at eight each evening.

They continued to address each other with formal
pronouns. Not out of politeness, they both knew that,
but because it prevented them from sliding into an
everyday rut.

After dinner one wet June evening, Armin laid two
plane tickets to San Francisco on the table. The flight
was in two days. "Don't forget to take your sax." She
grinned and scratched her leg. "Your pretty blue hair
is starting to grow out."

Before the trip she had her hair redyed. Actually, she
would have liked to do something else with it—but
better not take any risks. He knew her like that. So
let it stay that way.

. . .

Once they were on American soil, Armin spoke to her only in English. Fluent and no accent. He was lighter on his feet and laughed more often. Was he just fitting in with the Americans, or did he really feel different?

The air conditioners in the expensive hotels rumbled softly. Sometimes she felt like Jean Arthur, sometimes more like Lauren Bacall—she felt good.

Armin carried her saxophone around town, and when on their third day he spotted two black men standing on a street corner and playing tenor sax and guitar, he took it out of its case. Was she supposed to play? Armin begged her to, and the two blacks nodded good-naturedly. She was embarrassed. She thought she was playing much too straight and with no imagination. Armin took pictures. The childlike eyes of the two musicians. Suddenly, violent sharp cramps in her stomach that almost took her breath away. She felt like a fraud. A total fraud. That passed. People stopped and gawked appreciatively.

Armin invited the two musicians to dine with them. She wasn't hungry, felt hot and listless. In an awkward move she knocked over her wineglass. They both liked Armin. His composure. Meanwhile he gingerly took her wrist and held it fast for several minutes. She felt easier, and was able to orient herself better again.

On Ocean Front Walk in Venice. On the beach, under palm trees. Armin on roller skates. Laughed each time he fell. Playing like a little boy. Unimaginable in Munich.

At the Tropicana Motel, Anna reached for his arm during the night in her sleep and pulled him closer to her. She woke up frightened: Her old balance was gone. Her body was changing, her skin turning fidgety and electric, her heart pounding. She showered. Black cockroaches scurried hastily along the rim of the bathtub. Several drowned. Not what she intended, stupid, dangerous. Ridiculous. But she knew she couldn't undo the change. What was it? Some biochemical process?

From then on it took real strength not to constantly touch Armin. "Why are you so tense?" he asked, in English, at breakfast. English muffins and orange juice. What was "tense," what did he mean? She shrugged: "Let's go to the movies."

They saw *Sunset Boulevard*. How different it was to watch the films here, where they came from and belonged. Armin put his arm around her and drew her to him. For him, noncommittal pleasure, for her, suddenly pure torment. Keep your mouth shut, divulge nothing. A struggle not to fall into her fantasy of informal pronouns. An infatuated goose? He wouldn't renew her contract, would send her packing. Boring, not what he had expected of her.

In Chicago she had a little diamond nose-ring made for herself, which Armin deftly and almost painlessly pierced into her nostril with his own hands, after she had asked him to.

Despite all her efforts, she found herself yawningly boring, but he was enjoying her. For now. Back in Munich, he at once fell into his old, reserved elegance, and Anna suffered all the more from her emotion-laden frailty.

For her twenty-first birthday, a little red Fiat. She threw herself around his neck.

Just two weeks later, on September twentieth, for the first time, he didn't come home. At ten o'clock Anna's heart beat noticeably faster for about two minutes. Jean Seberg and Jean-Paul Belmondo soothed her for the next hour. A glass of Southern Comfort. Then suddenly a thick lump in her throat that made it difficult to swallow, and ice-cold hands. She paced, fear made breathing difficult. Never before had she been afraid for one second that he might have an accident or simply forget about her. At midnight she ran outside. Silence. When she tripped over a little rock and fell, she began to cry. The crying turned to gagging. She vomited, couldn't stop gagging. She crept back into the house on hands and knees, drew herself up into a ball on the bathroom rug. Every five minutes the gagging came back, passing through in great waves, jolting her. After each attack she tried to breathe calmly and relax. An effort. This would lead to something.

When Armin arrived around a quarter to seven, she was exhausted, but in control. He took a bath. Fresh coffee. His bright eyes, that calm, indifferent tone: "I'm sure you asked yourself why I didn't come home last night as always." She smeared quince jelly on a hard roll for him and affected a smile. "Yesterday I met a very unusual woman, an artist."

"Some more coffee?"

He nodded.

"I intend to offer this woman artist a contract similar to yours. Your contract will run for the full year . . . and of course you can continue to live here. Now, I don't want to just run right over you, Anna —would it bother you if this lady"—he took a bite of his roll—"moved in tomorrow?"

She gave him a wordless smile. Then a scream, high and about fifteen seconds long. He regarded her calmly, only slightly put off, took a swallow of coffee. Anna clapped her mouth shut, grinned and sat down on the arm of his chair.

"Well, you see," she said offhandedly, rubbing her hand over his chin, "I'm pregnant. In my third month. I don't know if you want the baby . . . most of all I need peace and quiet . . ."

His reaction to her lie exceeded her expectations. Joy. He hugged her, beamed, called his office to say he wasn't coming in. Champagne and oysters for the mother. After her second glass, Anna: "If you really want me to have the baby, I'd like you to draw up a contract promising that we'll live together—for the child's benefit—until it's grown. And maybe my salary could be raised to . . . twenty-eight hundred marks?" She giggled. From today on, she decided, she'd use the informal pronoun with him. My goodness, why was he so delighted by this baby? They gazed into each other's eyes in silence, and as Anna regarded her image mirrored in his pupils, it became clear to her that each only appeared to understand the other's language.

Pregnancy gave a decisive direction to her life from then on. She ate regularly and with the sense that it was for her own good—a pound of nuts by midmorning, two bars of chocolate, drank a pint of cream. A two-hour pause for digesting that, then spaghetti and navy beans at noon, sometimes, when she could bring herself to it, half a pound of butter, melted, with a little salt. In the afternoon, juices to stimulate her appetite and vitamins and more nuts. All this eating didn't repulse her. She wasn't sick to her stomach even once. Only after Armin arrived in the evening would she sometimes have to lie down, and he would sit down beside her and hold her hand.

He spent his nights with his unusual woman artist, but he would call Anna every hour and ask how she was doing. For the first time in her life, a feeling of calm and abiding strength. The diet took effect. Her face lost its sharp contours, grew broad and tranquil. All about it the tangle of blue hair. Her flesh was foreign to her in its ponderousness. Once she scared herself when she saw her figure in the entryway mirror and did not immediately recognize it as her own. The blue hair, the only part of her that stayed unchanged. Her clothes, more and more ample. Her growing heft pleased her. She could sense her bones, her flesh, her blood moving, and to her it felt like an accomplishment.

Pastel-blue and pink wool for the baby. Two different hues of jackets, pants and caps. Armin was amused.

Knitting—had never learned how. She had the woman at the wool shop advise her. She thrust her spine forward and bore her belly before her the way she'd seen pregnant women do. Mothers holding little children by the hand would give her friendly nods, Anna's peculiar hair seemed to matter less to them now.

Each morning, when Armin would shove a vitamin-and-calcium pill between her lips . . . he was so touchingly concerned about her. No, she didn't want to go to bed with him anymore—he had to understand that. To be precise, he had never actually asked it of her. Curious, but since she had become pregnant, she no longer felt any desire for him. The attention he was showing was enough for her. She said she wanted to visit the clinic by herself. Female matters.

The birth. Miscarriage maybe? She'd come up with something. There was the contract, or would it be invalid, if no baby . . . Worry about that later.

For hours on end she sat in the leather armchair, often doing nothing except let thoughts form in her brain, let them stroll about on the white wall opposite her, bounce off, and just as slowly let them wander back into her brain.

.  .  .

A December evening beside the fire. Armin massaged her legs. "Why don't you bring your friend, the artist, for coffee sometime? Why not tomorrow afternoon, sweetheart?!" She treated herself to pet names once in a while now, was allowed them, she noticed—as a mother.

His interest and his concern were directed at her belly, that was clear to her. But no head, no belly. No Anna, no child. "If it won't be too much for you, I'd be glad to invite her!" Who was he addressing when he used the informal pronoun these days? Her or the child already? Who cared? Okay, coffee and cake. The lady painter: red hair and nickel-rimmed glasses. Anna knitted. Conversation about a gallery opening. Abruptly, Anna flashed the painter a smile. Dreamily: "He's just so madly happy about the baby, you know . . ."

Armin took hold of Anna's wrist. She loosened herself amiably from his grip, was really so calm and secure. The lady painter nodded. Soon took her leave.

Armin did not blame Anna when he never heard from the painter again, and she disappeared the very next day to Italy or wherever.

He was now spending his nights at home again. They would snuggle close together on his bed and watch movies. Sometimes, to amuse Armin, Anna would turn the sound off and dub Jean Arthur and Cary Grant, Lauren Bacall and Humphrey Bogart herself. Beans every day made her belly taut and hard. He would use his hand to feel the baby moving. And in fact, it did move. Anna was radiant. At night she preferred to sleep alone. Lonely? Yes, sometimes, in the wee hours, when she would lie awake in bed, hitching up her nightgown to observe her empty, thick, white belly. But then in the morning, Armin: "How're we three doing this morning?" A mother's little smile, not too broad, not too radiant, pregnancy really was strenuous, you know. During the day, she waited. Never bored, because she thought of it as her job.

She had settled on March twenty-fourth as the date of birth. From February on, she spent the days in bed. No matter how much she ate, her belly wouldn't get any bigger. The fat went to her legs and arms. When she made circles with her arms, two thick folds formed at the wrists. Lard. It didn't disgust her, not then. Incomprehensible these days. Armin bought an expensive nineteenth-century cradle in an antique shop. Lost in thought, he would stand beside it, rocking it back and forth.

Early in March, Anna ordered diapers, bottles, a diapering table with a little bassinet, a scale and a two-pound jar of Nivea cream, all by telephone.

. . .

Armin spent his evenings turning her other room, which she had hardly used since quitting school, into a nursery. From her bed she could watch him through the door, hard at work. A cheerful pale yellow on the walls. Armin had changed, was no longer so totally unapproachable, was more receptive to normal and undramatic things. He made it possible for her to be pregnant. Nothing but pregnant.

If it was a boy she'd call him Jan, a girl, Angelika, fter her mother.

Photographs of birth in the magazines that Armin had subscribed to for her. Those little people, smeared with blood, unhappy grimaces on their faces. They had to love their mothers—they had no choice. Anna smiled to herself. A little, self-made boyfriend—or would she prefer a girlfriend? "Armin, what do you want—a girl or a boy?"

He sat down beside her on the bed. "Why can't I come to the clinic with you?" "I can fight better if you're not along, believe me." "And afterwards? After the birth?" "Oh, Armin, that's hard to explain. I want to get used to being a mother on my own first. Let me do it my way."

Of course, of course, he respected all her wishes. How open he was now. As if he grew younger with each day of waiting for the baby. And gentler. Back then, she had almost won.

The birth. Her heart pounded just at the word. Another three weeks until the date.

And then one afternoon, sitting in her armchair, the plan. Suddenly it was there. Her brain had engendered it without her even noticing, and had offered it to her. She had agreed to it at once.

On March twenty-second, Anna knew when she awoke that today was the day. She climbed out of bed and joined Armin in the bathroom. He was taking his morning bath. His eyes gave her a friendly greeting. Nothing was said. She passed her hand once over his hair. He permitted such gestures, though they were totally foreign to his nature.

She took out the little suitcase. Baby things in both pink and pastel blue, diapers, powdered milk, bottles. Comfortable traveling clothes for herself.

A note for Armin: "Labor pains, have gone to the clinic. Please don't try to find out which one—you promised. Everything will be okay. Anna."

She took the train to Frankfurt. It seemed the right choice: Not too far away, four hours by train, she knew no one there—so why not Frankfurt? The two old women in her compartment gave her friendly nods. She had to stop eating today. Not a single calorie would pass her lips, she vowed to herself. Just black tea—well, okay, some buttermilk, too. But otherwise, absolutely nothing. Right after giving birth your belly was still big. Everyone knew that. She'd have to buy a girdle, a tight dress. There were those slenderizing pills you could get in any drugstore. There was so much to do.

In Frankfurt, for the first night she got herself a comfortable hotel room with pink-flowered curtains. She couldn't sleep for hunger. The baby! In that moment she lost it. It starved to death inside her body. Baloney. Tears. For the first time since the beginning of her pregnancy, the tears of helplessness. She started out at ten o'clock with no breakfast. Head scarf, loose coat, sunglasses, suitcase in hand. The pedestrian zone was sure to be a good spot. She dared not look as if she were searching for something. She window-shopped, all the while watching the street out of the corner of her eye. How very few children there were!

Not until three-thirty, two baby-buggies. The one was watched over by an older sister, while the mother shopped inside; a dachshund was tied to the other one. A dog—no, she lacked the courage for that.

. . .

To be on the safe side, a different hotel each night. Her feet hurt.

Tuesday, Wednesday, Thursday it poured. Dizzy with hunger. The nights lonely.

At two a.m. she called Armin and with joy in her voice told him she'd had a healthy boy. What an idiot I am! But Armin: overwhelmed, happy. She quickly hung up. Friday, another entire day in the pedestrian zone. Nothing. Her stomach rebelled. She was seeing spots. She leaned against a wall. Who was she without a baby? Turning back was impossible. No Armin, no place to live, no money at some point. And the worst part: no sense to life.

She forced herself to be calm, more systematic. The birth notices in the paper. She checked off the boys. Foreign workers' babies were maybe not a bad idea . . . the parents were more helpless than Germans. Franco Martini and Kenan Ösaydin lived on the same street in Bockenheim. Got her courage back. She took a taxi there, waited in entryways. She was freezing, but she felt her determination grow within her. All that day neither Frau Ösaydin nor Frau Martini emerged from the house with their babies. She waited the next day, too. The suitcase with the baby things always beside her. Finally a little sun.

. . .

Frau Ösaydin—that had to be her—short, fat and wearing a head scarf, Kenan in her arms, a little bundle.

Along with two neighbors, Frau Ösaydin walked to the grocery on the corner. Suddenly Anna's heart was banging. Anna entered the shop, stood behind her. A sweet baby! "Could I . . . hold him?" Frau Ösaydin didn't understand. Anna spread her arms. Frau Ösaydin smiled, nodded and laid Kenan in Anna's arms. The neighbors nodded to Anna, said something, in Turkish? She tensed every muscle. Did the door swing in or out? And then she was running, Kenan clutched tightly to her. She was fast. Behind her shouts, then tramping feet. She heard gasps. Someone grabbed her by the coat, a woman with a red head. Anna turned as she ran and hurled the suitcase against the woman's stomach. She lost her scarf—damn, her blue hair— the woman buckled over, stopped. Anna kept running, pain in her side. Two blocks. A taxi. Catch her breath. Kenan kept mum. "Central Station, please." Sweet little Kenan. No, Jan. Jan.

Until time for the train, she sat with Jan in the ladies' room. Gave him his bottle, sang him some songs. A quiet baby. The blue knit jacket looked good on him. She put on some lipstick, tied a scarf around her head.

. . .

By the time the train reached Würzburg, Jan was almost her own baby. The memory of the days in Frankfurt was already dimming. Her brain was doing good work. It washed out the colors in the scenes she'd experienced, blurred their contours. Anna smiled. Jan held tight to her index finger. Strong. A fighter just like her.

On the trip home from the Munich train station, Jan slobbered a little on her shoulder as he slept. She had won. Her son. Her friend. She was happy.

Fathers are nuts. Completely nuts. Had Armin ever given her a look like that, such a tender, meltingly tender look as he now gave his son? Carefully, ever so carefully, he took Jan in his arms, kissed him.

"Black eyes and black hair like my grandfather's."

Anna smiled. Jan began to squall. A completely normal baby. No, she couldn't nurse him. No milk, that happens with a lot of women. Armin took her in his arms now, thanked her for this lovely, healthy child. "He's got my eyebrows, though, don't you think?" Yes, of course—he had Armin's eyebrows, she saw it now, too. He wanted to change Jan's diaper. Anna had to show him how. Thrilled, Armin felt Jan's arms and legs, the feet the size of his thumb, the plump belly with its umbilical knot. Good heavens, could it be Kenan had been circumcised . . . She noticed how her face was twitching. She would have liked to shove Armin aside. It was her baby. Hers alone.

For a long while Armin sat beside the cradle, gazing at his sleeping son. Anna stretched out beside them on her bed. First thing tomorrow, she'd have to dye her hair.

Later they drank a glass of wine together. Armin seemed more of a stranger to her than ever before. He caressed her, rewarded her, but the tokens of affection, so unlike him, did not reach her. She had Jan's warm odor of milk and Nivea cream in her nostrils. "I would never have believed how exciting a baby can be. I'd like to give him his bottle tonight." Anna wanted to argue. Her sleep wasn't important to her. She gave a little cough and leaned back. Now don't get jealous on him. There were at least sixteen years ahead with Jan and Armin. Why should she turn petty at this point?

Armin took a week off, had another dentist sub for him. He bathed, fed, diapered Jan and carried him around the house whenever he wasn't asleep. He annoyed Anna. The week would pass, then Jan would be hers again.

. . .

The bleaching powder had an acrid odor and tickled her nose. Amazing, how young she looked with blond hair. As if she were fifteen. She laughed at herself in the mirror.

Later, as she was walking through the center of the city, shopping for some new clothes, it bothered her that people no longer stared at her. She was like all the others now. Anna Blume, twenty-one years old, mother. She liked it. She could feel the resolution showing on her face. Jan, my darling—thank you. In a kiddie boutique she bought stacks of bright-colored baby things. A little red cap with a cute bill. Jan was going to be the wildest, most fantastic kid ever.

She sensed something was wrong even before she got in the house. Armin was sitting in the leather armchair in the living room. Pounding heart. Anna raced to Jan's room. He lay sleeping peacefully in his cradle. She kissed him carefully on his brow, and he grunted softly. She walked into her adjoining room; suddenly she felt her heart ache.

Armin was standing there at the door, his face calm and controlled, the way it used to be. "I was listening to the news. In Frankfurt a woman said to have blue hair kidnapped a Turkish baby. I have nothing to say, except this: I'll give you until ten o'clock tomorrow morning to give the child back. After ten, I'll see to it myself." He left the room. Anna was still sitting on her bed. A tantrum was pointless. She sat down beside the cradle. Turkish baby. What nonsense! Her Jan. Tears were streaming down her face, but she didn't feel them. She had to come up with something. Come up with something good. A contract . . . but what could she offer Armin? She had nothing left she could sell him. This man with no imagination. This rich ice-cube. His stupid, cool poise. She felt hot. Jan woke up, looked at her with his dark eyes, whimpered. She took him in her arms. His skin, his smell, that little head with its little, slowly growing brain. She stroked the soft down. My baby. And she was supposed to give up her plan for their lives for the next sixteen years? What idiot could demand that of her? She locked the door. About one o'clock she heard Armin go to his room. A little later she slipped into the kitchen to warm Jan's milk for him. Her bare feet on the cold tiles, her arms crossed. The house was completely silent. And when she imagined how it would be if only just she and Jan were in the house . . . She put the bottle to her lips to test the temperature.

Jan suckled contentedly, batting his eyelashes with each gulp. He held on to her. Anna smiled at him.

.    .    .

She didn't sleep all night. Every muscle hurt. She sat beside Jan's cradle and stared out the window. She would have loved to play her saxophone now—it used to help her to think things over. Woman with blue hair, playing the saxophone. No, that wasn't her anymore at all. She tried to imagine Armin lying asleep there in the next room, but she couldn't even think of what his face looked like. As if a heavy veil were draped over it. She made several attempts to recall his nose, his eyes, his mouth, until she realized that her brain was intentionally covering Armin's face. Of course. As the sky outside grew slowly brighter, her muscles relaxed, she felt rested and fresh. But of course. Now she knew how, too. Quietly she left her room. Armin would be getting up in a half hour. Get a move on, but no need for haste.

The hair dryer lay on the top shelf of the little cupboard in the bathroom. The nail scissors. The nail scissors. She couldn't find them, fetched a sharp kitchen knife. The insulation had to go. She cut it back all the way around, a half-inch from where the wires entered the dryer's plastic case. It had been such a modern mini-hair dryer. She laid the dryer back in the cupboard, carried the kitchen knife to the kitchen and returned to the nursery.

. . .

She waited, not moving at all. Don't think anymore now. She felt her heart grow lighter.

Armin got up punctually, and, as he did every morning, ran the water in the tub for his bath while he shaved. Another five minutes. She kissed Jan before she left.

Armin lay in the water. They didn't look at each other. She washed her hair at the sink. She massaged the shampoo into her scalp as she gazed at herself in the mirror. A pretty face, would stay pretty for at least ten years. The water turned yellowish when she rinsed her hair. The blue hair was to blame for that. To blame for everything. She took the dryer from the cupboard. Armin was splashing behind her, soaping himself. Careful, the wire. She plugged it in and turned the dryer on. It began to purr softly. She was still looking in the mirror as she let the dryer fall, with a sudden graceful motion, into the bathtub. A big wave slopped over the rim, onto the carpet, getting everything wet. She looked at the floor, saw Armin's ugly jerking out of the corner of her eye. No sound. She had expected a scream. Nothing. Just the jerking. Went on and on. She looked back in the mirror. Her blue eyes almost black now. The sloshing water calmed down only very slowly. Minutes passed before she turned back around. His mouth open, distorted. Luckily no blood. She pulled the plug out, briefly catching her own eyes in the mirror as she did so. Blue. Bright blue. There, you see. She carefully lifted the hair dryer from the water by its cord, dried it and laid it back in the cupboard.

Anna felt very grown-up as she went into the kitchen to fetch Jan's bottle. She yawned. Jan lay, eyes open wide, in his cradle, and it seemed to her that he had smiled before she even came through the door. Soon he would learn to say "Mama." In how many months? They had so much time.

When Jan had drunk his bottle, she put a fresh diaper on him and put him back to bed, called the doctor. The heart, the heart. Police never set foot in the house.

She managed quite well with the 2,800 marks that were transferred automatically to her account each month. Anna and Jan had modest demands. She stroked his head gently.

# Men

It was late. He couldn't bring himself to go home. For a half hour now he had been trying to dictate a letter, but his thoughts kept wandering further and further afield. He stood up and regarded himself critically in the cabinet mirror: Julius Armbrust, early forties. His suit sat well, he looked fresh and energetic. Not handsome, but interesting, and by now he had learned that women went for interesting more than for handsome. On the whole he could truly say that he was a good-looking man, one who radiated a certain amount of power—"potency" was the word that occurred to him. Why the hell had this had to happen to him, then?

He sat back down.

"On the basis of our long experience, may we urge you to package your product in cardboard boxes. Period. Renate, would you please finish this silly letter for me? We want the contract, so tie a pretty ribbon around it." He let out a short laugh. "I'd like to tell you about something . . . well, actually I want to ask you something. There's this man I know, he's been married almost twenty years now. Nice wife, maybe a little too suburban a glint in the eyes for your taste. Nice kids. Nice house—well, you've got the picture, about like with me. They both certainly had no illusions about eternal love, or the grand passion, but they did pretty nicely together in bed, even after fifteen years, they got along, there was money enough . . . You see, I simply don't understand, that's the problem, I can't get it into my head . . ."

Julius stopped the dictaphone, removed the cassette, angrily ripped the tape out and unreeled it into the wastebasket.

She had told him about it over three-minute eggs at breakfast, not confessed, simply told, the way she was in the habit of commenting on some news story she had just read. The night before he had watched her undress, and had thought to himself, the flesh is getting flabby, my dear.

Was the same age he was, she said. Name? Unimportant. Occupation? She didn't know exactly, something in the artistic line, she hadn't asked him, the most important thing after all was that . . . That he was good in bed? After that, she had had nothing more to say about him.

Good, to be fair, he needed to keep in mind his own countless affairs with secretaries, consultants and assistants, but there was a big difference there, because he knew quite well how little those brief, sultry dalliances had meant to him; for her, he was sure of that, it was quite another thing, something more profound.

It was hot, the city swept empty, school was out, the kids on their way to Greece and Italy. He missed them terribly, in the foolish assumption that they could have helped comfort him a little.

He didn't understand why every bone in his body ached, since he had, after all, considered the possibility, had often asked himself, when she was being particularly tender and soft, if she'd just come from seeing another man.

Paula, my little housewife, was what he called her in his mind. She had nothing in common with the cool chic of the women who surrounded him on the job, there was something slightly rumpled about her, which he often found touching, but she had class, style.

His specialty was packaging, an asinine profession, he thought so himself, the bozos of industry, but that suited him, he could be very funny and liked being

the center of attention. He designed packaging con-
cepts, and the salary he earned—with plastic bags for
peanuts he would never eat himself, with collapsible
boxes, vacuum cans and yogurt containers—seemed
incongruously large, and for years now he had felt a
certain disdain for a world that let its packages cost
so much.

They're sitting at dinner, and he takes note of her
white arms, the creases at her wrist, the delicate
freckles, the short pink-lacquered fingernails, and suddenly he hates those plump little hands, that innocent
pink in particular, he pictures her hands on some
strange male flesh, they look deceitful and homicidal
to him. He has to get up, looks at her from behind,
her broad, firm back, her full, auburn hair, from the
rear she's still young and pristine, so damned pristine.
He doesn't really like her, no, he does not like her.
Relieved, he sits back down—and loves her more
than anything.

A chance to attend a convention in Frankfurt turns
up. He takes it, even though he doesn't feel like it,
but he has to get out of the house, or he will suffocate.
Not because he has been wounded, but because she
is being so meek, almost apologetic. It's all his fault,
for carrying on like a jealous husband out of another
century. As always, she packs his suitcase for him.

Backing out the door, he sees her standing in the depths of the room, her arms dangling helplessly, and with painful accuracy he suddenly recalls all the rooms he has ever shared with her, that crummy little hotel room where it all began, all the apartments that have grown bigger and posher over time, and it seems to him now as if the distance between them has grown along with them, as if they are fated to end in a cold, dark palace, she at the window and he at the door, miles apart, and not a single human voice can find its way through those chambers.

For two hours he drove around the city, with no purpose or goal, and then returned to their trim house in the suburbs, parked the car around the corner and hid himself across the street behind the hedge in the Feichingers' yard—they were out of town. He feels like a stupid little kid who's hidden himself so well for hide-and-go-seek that no one can find him, and his heart starts pounding because their shouts are getting weaker and weaker: Julius! Julius, where are you? until they stop altogether, and everybody figures he'll show up sooner or later, but no, that'll never happen, he'll starve behind the hedge, and hot tears run down his cheeks.

The other guy drives an old Beetle, wears jeans and has longish hair, a nebbish, an aging nebbish, a nobody in a bright blue VW. From this distance you might think Frau Armbrust from across the street was being picked up by her son for a trip into town, it's almost touching, he's taking Mom for a ride, and she's calmly ignoring his shabby outfit. (How can anybody pushing forty still look like that?) But she's in his arms, her dress hiked up to reveal a pair of sturdy, white legs, Paula can't handle sun, and he's certain she smells of the Eau de Joy he gave her. The door on the passenger side is hard to open, she jiggles at it and lets out a childish laugh, a laugh that doesn't suit her, it's too loud, and he, her-son-the-college-kid, tosses her a smile.

In Frankfurt Julius makes a mistake. She is in her mid-thirties maybe and a consultant for one of their competitors, tall, slender and athletic, which he can't stand, she laughs and talks with everyone but all the while keeps her cool distance. He catches up with her in the hotel lobby, ties her up in some shop talk that she breaks off with a smile saying she's had enough for today, he feels like he's being clumsy and pushy, and so he can't let her get away now, he invites her to dinner, she declines, he keeps pressing her, won't let loose, ends up begging her, which annoys him all the way through the meal, although she is charming and indulgently keeps the small talk going just so he can have a chance to regain his composure. Which doesn't improve things, just the opposite, he's got one notion in his head, and slowly it begins to poison him; he's going to get her into his bed tonight.

She doesn't resist, and that's the really god-awful part about the situation. She has asked him to leave, but she doesn't go hysterical or prudish on him when he pounces on her with unbridled kisses, she merely stares at him with infinite boredom, and then he can't even do it, and she lends a helping hand, it has two jingling gold bracelets. He could murder her for that, but she even puts up with it, hands him the Kleenex, and now what he'd like most is to ask her to put him to bed and stay with him until he's fallen asleep.

That night was the first time he dreamed about the fish. It lay in a bed of roses, a large, gray, carplike fish, its skin was all scraped bloody and it was still gasping weakly for air. Julius bent down over it and picked it up, with an effort, it was a good deal heavier than it looked. Its eyes gaped blindly, it lay limp in Julius's arms as he carefully bore it from the garden, it grew heavier and heavier, the Feichingers, the Küppers, the Sticker kids were standing behind the fence whispering and pointing at him. He muttered something to comfort the fish and desperately tried to recall in what direction the sea lay. An endless highway stretched before him, trucks thundered past, the fish was so heavy now that he could barely carry it, he trudged on, ending up in muck and mire, and at every step he had to fight back the idea of simply tossing the fish behind the next shrub. He had the feeling that he dare not fail this time, that he had to complete this task, to do everything absolutely right just this once, and obediently he kept on going.

Since he has nothing more to lose with her, the next day he asks her to do him a favor. She is wearing an elegant gray dress, is cool and friendly, will forgive him nothing, but neither does she remind him of the embarrassment of last night. Sure, she writes down the message for him in a somewhat impersonal, too-pretty hand: Julius, darling. Forgive me for not contacting you. Please call me the next time you're in town.

He suggests she sign it Sandra, but she talks him into Gabriele. It should be something restrained, that would make it more believable. She even gives him one of her pastel-blue envelopes, addresses it with his home address just as he requests, thrusts the letter into his hand and dismisses him without a word.

Three days later he is slinking around his own house like some stranger, then searches Paula's desk for that stupid, pastel-blue love letter and doesn't find it. The house smells different, or so he imagines, smells of HIM. There is no sound, he looks at his feet to see if his shoes have left dirty tracks on the pale velour carpet; he could simply lie down on his bed and wait for her, he could sit in his favorite armchair, the one his kids disappear from without his so much as asking whenever they see him coming, newspaper in hand, he could have a look at the roses, go through the mail, he could . . .

He leaves.

It's a cheap pension on the edge of town, because he's afraid that in an expensive, downtown hotel he may meet people he knows, and besides Paula might find his car. The flowers running riot in the wallpaper of his room make him dizzy. There is no television. What is he doing here? Is he going to drive to work from here every morning? Paula would try to call him there every day. He has nothing to say. He wishes that with one fell swoop he could stop loving her, or love her much more than he probably does.

He doesn't have to fake it, he does in fact get sick. His landlady, a plump, good-natured woman, calls in at work for him. He refuses to see a doctor, accepts the cold compresses she makes for him and sinks eagerly into a fever. At one point he imagines Paula standing beside his bed and bending over him. He wants to hold on to her, whisper to her that she should send that stupid college kid packing, wants to laugh with her about the whole affair, just laugh it all away.

The landlady helps him out of bed and to the john.

In the mirror he sees an old, gaunt man. His hair is hanging down over his ears—how long has he been in this damn pension? His nose protrudes in a point from his face, his skin is yellow and wrinkled, success and power have fallen away, that's quite obvious.

He dreams about the fish again. He's warm, the fish is slimy-cold, and he ponders how he can transfer his own body heat to the fish, and as he dreams he thinks, how stupid, it's perfectly normal for a fish to be so cold.

After three weeks he can get up for the first time. His expensive tailored suits hang on him like sacks, but it isn't just his body that no longer fits them, his face doesn't seem to want to belong to them anymore, either.

Paula now seems like some fictional character, someone he has thought up. But why has his imagination led him to fall for this particular woman? Not a striking beauty, always a little too heavy, stubborn and sometimes almost scathingly self-assured.

While he is struggling to shave his beard, still believing that he is to blame for this total transformation, the pain returns, ever so slowly, but he can feel it seeping into his body again, and he finds it more unpleasant than his long illness.

.   .   .

He decided not to go back home, or at least not like this; in triumph, if at all. But what was there to win? He sat down on the bed and stared at the hideous flowered wallpaper that in his fevered dreams had sometimes looked like a billowing floral sea, and suddenly he thought he could see hidden within it the essence of his life—that stuff had appeared in his visions because he couldn't bear it in its banality. It dawned on him that everything about him, about his marriage, about Paula, about his children was so normal it stank, and suddenly that thought was more painful than anything else.

He had to set Paula's mind to rest. The letter proved an effort: "Dear Paula, as you've probably guessed, I'm in over my head in a wild affair. Nothing serious—we're almost at a parting of the ways, okay? Don't worry . . . I still don't know exactly when I'll be coming home. Let's spend a nice summer together. Everything is back to normal. A kiss from your old Julius, right on your favorite spot."

He drove two hundred miles to the next major city to mail the letter. He would do battle like a knight of old, and the idea pleased him.

For the present, he decided to stay on at the pension. He sold his car for fear he'd give himself away otherwise. He rode through the city on his bike, past her beauty salon, her bank, her favorite restaurant, past the dress shop she liked, never resting, till he was exhausted.

Paula was sitting with HIM in a café, and Julius gave her credit for picking a spot where she had never been with him. She had a new hairdo, he was wearing jeans and a wrinkled shirt, as usual. They were holding hands, exchanging casual kisses that betrayed both habit and intimacy. Julius watched as she paid for them both, and a wave of blind hate welled up in him.

Twice he saw someone from his firm, but they passed by without noticing him, it was as if he had suddenly donned a cloak that made him invisible. Had they already cleaned out his desk, dumped the photographs of Paula and the kids and the drawings he made during long-winded calls into a plastic bag? In reality, he no longer existed, and for the first time in weeks, he grinned, touching the corners of his mouth it felt so strange.

The two met almost every day. Usually Paula picked him up in her Rabbit (wrong—it was his Rabbit, which he had given to her on her thirty-fifth birthday), sometimes they drove out into the country, or so he supposed, because he'd soon lose track of them and be left hanging on a road leading out of town. They often went to restaurants, to the movies. Never to his place, Julius's bed was softer presumably, but she would often let him off in front of an art-nouveau building, and Julius had a vivid picture in his mind of the apartment, old-fashioned, immense, and slightly run-down. They would share long kisses in the car. Julius endured it all until that last final embrace.

He often tried to imagine Paula alone in their house, but he never succeeded. What did she do there all alone? In his memory there were only scenes of them both together, and he would have liked to watch her in her solitude, played with the idea of creeping through the yard at night and peering in the window, but he was afraid he might get caught and lose sight of her face for good.

He made it a rule to pedal past the apartment house at least three times a day, and so it happened that he was watching once from across the street as the "college kid," as he called him, carried furniture and boxes of books out onto the street for a woman of about thirty, who then loaded them into a VW bus. When she started crying, Julius had a good idea who the woman was, and that with her exit some clear signals had been set.

Julius gave every one of his suits to the Goodwill, bought himself some old, faded jeans at a flea market, loud, cheap shirts, sneakers, his hair hung almost to his shoulders by now, he stopped shaving, something he found most unpleasant. When he looked at himself in the mirror then, he almost burst into tears, so chillingly and clearly aware was he of his own absurdity. If it weren't for his face, he could almost have convinced himself that he had not experienced the past twenty years, for this was how he had looked when he had chucked his course at the art academy and thrown himself lustily into the world of smartly cut suits and standards. He had no problem adapting, on the contrary, he set about purposefully learning the new rules with the ambition of an actor, and since he wasn't any more himself in sneakers and jeans than he had been with tie and credit cards, the notion of betrayal never entered his mind.

From now on he moved about without getting dizzy. He never let the guy out of his sight, followed him to the want-ad desk of a local paper and was apparently the first to apply: Room avail. in large apt., 380 DM, util. incl., call Stefan, 772561. The name turned his stomach.

Had Paula showed Stefan old family snapshots maybe? No, that lacking in taste she wasn't, and since Julius would hardly have recognized himself, he gave it no further thought.

It was indeed a large, bright, old-fashioned apartment, his room even had a little balcony. He acquired a mattress and enjoyed the feeling of owning nothing, of staring at white walls and of not being himself. He felt like a man in exile.

Stefan was friendly and yakked too much. Julius would have loved to strike him dead, but instead he watched him, greatly amazed, and could not imagine Paula in his arms.

His second day there, he listened for Stefan to go to the bathroom, pulled on his shorts and, as if he hadn't noticed the bath was occupied, flung open the door. Good, he was perhaps more muscular than Julius, hairier (hadn't Paula always remarked at the beach how she couldn't stand those hairy apes?), but otherwise he really didn't have much to offer. Julius felt relieved, muttered "sorry" and vanished into his room.

Stefan insisted on a "communal life," and so they ate late breakfast together, watched TV and cooked dinner for themselves. Julius didn't have to ask Stefan anything, he observed him very coolly and formed his own idea of him. Stefan, on the other hand, pumped him dry with questions.

During long, sleepless nights, Julius had worked out the details of his biography. Formerly an art instructor, later considerable success as a free-lance graphic artist, now unemployed and new in town, he had to make some changes, do some backtracking, start all over again. "A love affair that didn't work out?" Stefan asked knowingly. "Yes, that, too," Julius admitted, a good many things had not turned out right.

He had deliberately picked a professional background with an artistic slant to it—after all, that was the only thing that he knew about Stefan, and he had guessed right, because he took the bait at once, his training had been in graphic design and he was now employed as a magazine illustrator.

Stefan complained at length about how hard it was to get commissions in this rotten market, and how tired he was of conforming to the tastes of his mediocre art director. Julius replied that conforming was half of life, you just had to regard it as a kind of athletic competition. Stefan's sniveling, his lamentations over his lost utopia, got on his nerves. "What utopia?" Julius asked. "That of a better world, of a world that doesn't function solely by the rules of capitalism." "A world where the failures are secretly the winners, right? Because they're the 'better' people?" They argued into the wee hours, until Stefan admitted that his big dream was a Porsche.

As Julius lay in bed, watching how the gray walls were slowly dyed pink by the rising sun and then finally turned a sober white again, a thought emerged, foggy at first, but then as if on fast-forward it congealed and finally formed a clear, simple idea. He fell asleep.

Whenever Stefan left the house, Julius was sure that it was to meet Paula, but he squelched the urge to follow him. He wandered through the apartment,

searched Stefan's room, turned up his nose at his
sketches, happened on a shoe box of old photographs
that could just as easily have belonged to him. Stefan
at demonstrations, in communes, in Greece, from fifteen, sixteen years ago maybe, a smooth baby-face,
framed by carefully shampooed hair, girls on his arm,
every one of whom looked older than he, and Julius
was reminded of Paula, whom he had met at a university blowout; she lost her hairpiece necking, he
could see her earnest face before him, usually under
a layer of thick pink paste that he later talked her out
of; her dream was to save the world, which he had
found touching.

He had never really felt at home with the other
students, he had been a clown without political conscience, but in his conversations with Stefan he would
drop the pivotal names from those days, so that Stefan
was convinced that he had served the old "struggle,"
too, and together they drank to the decline of their
ideals. Julius was touched by Stefan's naive candor.
Like a dog, Stefan would wag his tail at every friendly
gesture. Julius quite obviously impressed him as a man
of the world who had voluntarily renounced prestige
and luxury to avoid being swallowed up by commerce.
He let Stefan believe it, even enjoyed the admiration,
but it made him feel strangely sad, too, and he did
not quite understand why.

When he spoke about himself, about the new Julius,

he admired the fellow's plain, incorruptible conduct, the man knew what he wanted, seemed to have an exact sense of himself. Julius began to fret over his new existence, in contrast to which his old one seemed shabby and corrupt, he didn't like the morality of this new gentleman, but he had no choice except to endorse and defend it.

He began to cook for Stefan and urge him on to work harder. He brought tea to his room, where he found him bent over his sketches, and encouraged him. He was surprised himself at how earnestly he meant it sometimes, how sincere his concern for Stefan was, when in reality he considered him as useless as a pimple to be squeezed and gotten rid of. "Am I growing fond of him?" He was shocked by the thought. "Is there a pimple on my heart?"

He felt tainted by Stefan's presence, and challenged him to work out with him, and from then on they went out "to play" as they called it, like little boys, they ran around several blocks for three quarters of an hour, wrestled on the lawn, almost tenderly, although the thought did occur to Julius sometimes to drop Stefan with a knockout punch.

He was annoyed by Stefan's lackadaisical indecisiveness and his relative freedom from all the constraints he himself was used to, and sometimes being around him felt just like when his sons, who had driven him crazy by sleeping till noon, would hang around the living room and read comics. He felt threatened by the chaos, and he set up a rigid schedule for Stefan, critiqued his sketches and advised him to be more courageous, more impudent, yes, more of a clown.

He taught him contempt.

Stefan blossomed under his hand. He dressed more meticulously, observed a healthier diet, grew more diligent, and his outlook improved. He now had less time for his "twosome" as he put it. Julius asked no questions, he was sure that at some point Stefan would unfold his whole love life to him, and he awaited that moment with nervous anticipation.

And yet he was unexpectedly wounded by Stefan's request that he go see a movie this Tuesday and then maybe spend an hour or two in a bar, for decorum's sake, because his current "relationship"—and Julius could have slapped him for that word—insisted on seeing how he lived.

He wanders the streets, unable to sit longer than ten minutes in a bar, having purchased a bottle of whiskey in the last one; he keeps circling closer to Stefan's apartment, picturing to himself in savage scenes of revenge how he will surprise them both in bed, stab Stefan, give Paula a thrashing and finally put an end to this farce.

What in fact prevents him from doing it is the vision of Paula's reaction—she would look at him calmly, maybe even smile, and say: Julius, cut the comedy.

It had taken a long time before she had unmasked him, unmasked was the wrong word maybe, for to this day, he stubbornly stuck to his story, although he had absolutely no proof for it. When he was little he had been accused of telling "fibs," he himself definitely preferred the term "rich imagination," and indeed, in his profession had constantly found confirmation for it: "That Armbrust is one imaginative guy." For his first girlfriend, he had played the poor orphan, until one day she saw him shopping with his mother. Later, for Paula, he had given his tales a more sophisticated and charming turn, he was, to be sure, a highly talented art student, but he had dropped out and turned on, with contacts to K-1 and scads of women and all his fantasies told of one helluva fireball, who nevertheless in his heart was an outsider, a lone wolf. It wasn't all that much of a distortion, really, for so carefully had he gone about inventing such traits, that at some point he believed them himself and acted on them, although at the same time he also knew that his whole life was built on bluff. He was simply quicker than the others, let his hair grow before anyone else did, was the first to travel to Algeria and barter his nylon shirts for hash, had such sovereign command of the latest political jargon that he came dangerously close to being elected department spokesman, and noted with amazement the consequences of his chameleon-like soul: he became one helluva fireball.

With time, since he didn't take himself seriously, he found he had forfeited every real sentiment, and he despised those who had not, people like Stefan, for instance, or Paula, too, who really had nothing at all to offer. That was a cheap shot, and he was immediately ashamed of thinking it.

He doesn't return until early morning and finds Stefan in the kitchen, in the doldrums.

"Well, have a great time?" Julius manages to ask.

"You'll never believe it. We sat here the entire evening and she told me all about her husband."

"About her husband?"

"Yes, a successful, bourgeois shithead."

"Oh. And what else?"

"I don't remember. What do I care about her husband? He's running around having an affair with some woman."

"Well," Julius hears himself saying, "then everything's hunky-dory. Or ... or is she still in love with him?"

"No, I don't think so. He's a poop, although, come

to think of it, she said that awfully sweetly. Must be pretty much of an asshole."

"Why's that?"

"She seems so starved . . . as if she hadn't had a man in her bed for the last twenty years, that's why."

"Aha. And now . . . now she's in love with you?"

"Maybe. I don't know. But she's so damn sure of herself, no doubts whatsoever . . ."

"Yes, that's her."

"What do you mean by that?"

"Oh, it sounds about right. Given the way she's jerking you around."

"You think so, too, huh? She decides when I can see her, when we . . . and she's so fucking suburban."

"So what do you want from her?"

"I can't explain. It's almost embarrassing, but I think she's the woman I want to spend my life with."

"What sort of a life would you have with her?"

"You got it. That's where it's at."

"I mean, that's not your world."

"But it could be."

"Never," Julius says flatly and makes Stefan some coffee.

"You know what, she says I'm so shy and modest, so straight-arrow and . . . a man from another planet."

"Sounds gruesome."

"Yeah, sure does. Sounds impotent if you ask me."

. . .

Julius stirs two teaspoons of sugar into Stefan's coffee for him. How could Paula fall for this dreary failure? Maybe because he was a failure? Alright, then he was not going to be one anymore. . . .

That night, he dreamed once more about the fish, finding it in the rose bed again, lifted it and recognized it at once as his fish, but this time it was light as a feather. He turned around, standing there in his yard and looking up at Paula in the window, she nodded to him, expected him to save the fish, and now he suddenly knew in what direction the sea lay, and he walked slowly through the yard and out onto the street.

The next day, Julius telephoned to make an appointment with the head of P.R. for one of his competitors, telling him he was sending over a good, and very talented, friend. Why didn't he drop in himself, because word was out that he had chucked his job, but before he can ask any more questions, Julius begs him to keep his own name out of it, he's got personal reasons, and hangs up. He knows the fellow from some carousing they've done together and he's tried over and over to lure Julius away, finally dubbing him "Mr. Stonewall."

. . .

Together with Stefan, he assembles a portfolio of sketches, writes him a letter of recommendation, praising him in the highest tones, finding just the right words for his spontaneity, effervescent imagination and his difficulty in conforming "artistically." That's important, you don't dare be uncomplicated, you're an artist after all, with a sensitive soul.

But when he sees Stefan standing there before him, in jeans and wrinkled shirt, portfolio under his arm, Julius knows that he has no chance whatever, it's that look he has about him, as if he's apologizing before he even starts.

He drags him to a men's clothing store and talks him into something expensive, but chic in a slightly wacky way. A dyed leather jacket, beneath it a very plain shirt, linen trousers, nicely wrinkled after five minutes, looking as if you've been hard at work, but not all that hard.

Julius pays for the leather jacket. Stefan is grateful. In front of the mirror he practices a couple of "Bozo numbers" with him, as he calls them, how to be loose, witty, as if you didn't need this, those guys in their boring offices need entertaining, let's face it, you have to promise them some excitement, since that's what they lack most.

Once he has finally got Stefan out of the house and is standing there alone in front of the mirror, in his jeans, his shabby T-shirt, those god-awful long bangs in his eyes, he is suddenly seized by an inexplicable fit of weeping. It jolts him, he lies down in a fetal position on the floor and can't seem to stop sobbing. He cries his whole life away, all those images he's made for himself, and when the weeping finally eases up, he feels a burden lifted, young and old at the same time.

Stefan got a well-paying position in the advertising department and threw himself with verve into his job. With never-ending amazement, Julius watched this metamorphosis. He soon started nagging Julius to finally go out and get himself a new job and stop hanging around the apartment like a frustrated housewife.

They saw each other only seldom, although Julius religiously had breakfast ready by seven each morning, so that he could observe the change in Stefan and perhaps channel it into the right path, but that wasn't necessary, for with the surefootedness of a sleepwalker, Stefan became an almost overnight success, a man in the prime of life who knows what he wants from the world and admits no doubts. Of course, he had less time for Paula now, and from time to time he'd let a remark fall like: A man shouldn't waste too much time and thought on women, they aren't worth the energy, and with women, the bottom line always turns out to be zip.

Julius was repelled more and more by this new man, and he had trouble keeping himself under control.

The night before Stefan disclosed to him that he was going to move into a new apartment, a large, expensive place with a terrace, in the ritziest part of town, Julius dreamed once again of his fish. He was heading for the sea, the fish had grown unbearably heavy, every step was torture, but, certain that he could soon return the fish to its element and thereby save his own life, Julius trudged on through the sand toward the water. When he looked down at his arms, to say good-bye to the fish, his hands were empty, the fish had vanished, but the unbearable weight was still there. In an attack of pure desperation and utter panic, he shook his arms to rid himself of the weight. It did no good. He remembered something, in school he had learned about somebody or other with some gold in a bathtub, and slowly he walked into the sea, submerged both arms in the water, and at that moment they grew lighter, the dragging weight disappeared, and suddenly, overjoyed, he swam out.

Their good-byes are cool and matter-of-fact. Actually, they want to go out for a last dinner together, but Stefan doesn't have the time, he is meeting the woman in charge of the layout department, Julius understands and hasn't the least regrets. Nothing connects him with this man anymore, he has won. He would like to let out a whoop of victory, if only as a matter of form, to raise his fist, to leap in the air, but stands there with arms hanging down and not a sound passes his lips.

He writes Stefan a couple of lines saying good-bye, it's been great, and lots of success and thanks, etc. He burns it, leaving it as a sentimental pile of ashes in a saucer, which he then puts on Stefan's desk. It's been great? He must have been crazy.

He goes to the barber, has his hair and beard cut and suspiciously eyes his own metamorphosis. He is not quite sure whether he ought to be happy to see the old Julius, something has been lost somehow, all of a sudden everything seems so serious, and he shakes himself like a dog as he leaves the shop.

He buys new clothes, a trace more serious and less chic than before, and when the clerk tries to suggest "something with a more youthful touch," he bellows at him to keep his tastes to himself.

He can't ride up on a bicycle . . . he walks, and since he feels foolish strolling down the street with his little suitcase in hand, he sets it down behind a hedge.

Paula's reception is friendly, calm, the children's, ditto. After a few minutes everything is just the same as always. Paula is on the phone with a friend, the kids have got the music turned up too loud, Julius is sitting in his armchair asking himself what he had best do now. He sees himself, sitting there with his legs crossed, as a man waiting for something, he feels out of place.

That night they lie quietly beside each other, holding hands, very cautiously Julius asks Paula about HIM, how the two of them are doing.

"Oh, you know," Paula says, and at one time she would now have edged very close to him, "you know, I thought he was so very different. . . ."

"Different how?"

"Well you know, a man from another star, no house, no family, no worries about success or taxes, someone who is totally free . . . But now he's got a job with Weber and Company, right, what a laugh, them of all people, and wham! he's just like all the rest, too. . . ."

"Like me, you mean?" Julius asks, barely managing to get it out.

"No, not in the least like you. You at least don't take it seriously. What's up with your job by the way? They've been dialing their fingers raw trying to reach you. Were you so much in love, that you didn't even—"

"At the start, maybe," Julius interrupts her, "but

then I found out she was just all fluff, totally empty inside, a pretty little thing, nothing more."

"Very young, huh?"

"No, about your age."

"I don't know whether that makes it better or worse."

Julius takes her in his arms and looks over her shoulder at his suit hanging on the chair like wrinkly molted skin.

"What are you thinking about?" she asks, her head on his chest.

"Oh, I was just thinking about what to wear in the morning."

"You have the dandiest, normalest thoughts, sweetheart."

# Money

Carmen Müller, thirty-five years old, married to Werner Müller for fourteen years, two half-grown children, Karin and Rainer, with a house, a car, television and VCR, a deep-freeze, but no vacation for five years now and debts galore. Carmen Müller, cleaning lady with fourteen years experience, she thought to herself as she wiped up the flooded bathroom where a hose on the washing machine had burst during the night, while Karin aloofly scrambled over her, heading for the mirror and ardent application of her makeup.

*I am my children's employee.*

Meanwhile in the kitchen, the coffee maker was boiling over, which Rainer, age thirteen, seemed to take not the least notice of. He was sitting at the breakfast table, reading, and said without glancing up: "Ma, get dressed for cryin' out loud."

. . .

*I'm a jellyfish. Fat and flabby. My children are ashamed of me. I don't know how other women do it. I don't mind being ugly if it helps make my kids look even better. Werner isn't exactly an Adonis either, but we managed to have two gorgeous kids. That's something, isn't it?*

Werner was still lying in bed. For seventeen years now he had worked as a foreman in a toy factory, supervising the conveyor belts, and Carmen could well understand how he had gradually lost interest in that and found it harder and harder to get out of bed. She slathered three rolls for him, just as she did every morning, one for breakfast and two for work, and admired her impeccable, trendy children, dressed as always to a fare-thee-well in the latest fashions, expensive and elegant, and here came the magical sentence: "Pop, all the kids at school are wearing like these new moccasins . . ." and Carmen knew that, despite her weak objection of "You just bought new sweaters last week," she would get nowhere, and there was Werner already fumbling with his wallet.

Werner could never refuse the children anything, he had a soft heart, too soft, or so Carmen often thought, but she loved him, and the only thing she ever really had held against him was his last name. Carmen Müller, it just sounded tacky, your basic nice-try-but-no-cigar.

"You kids are spoiled worse than any I know," she said, shaking her head.

"Well, you two," Karin replied, "could do a little better job keeping yourselves up. Pop, you're getting fat, and Ma, your hair's turning gray. Why don't you just go ahead and dye it?" With that, they stood up and dashed off.

As she was packing his sandwiches in his satchel, Carmen said to Werner: "You know, sometimes I wish they had pimples on their noses or greasy hair or . . ."

"Yes," Werner said, "sometimes I ask myself if they're really mine. . . ."

Carmen took him in her arms. "No cure for old age or beauty." She shoved him out the door.

*This is the nicest time of the day, when they're all gone and I'm alone with you. I make me some coffee, the way I like it, real strong, not that dishwater I make for Werner and his weak heart, and when I sit back down at the breakfast table, I can always redd it up later, there's a whole different family sitting here, my husband is tall and slim, he's so good-looking all the women are after him, but I don't have to worry, he loves only me, his wife, pretty as a picture, who's still got the figure of a young girl, itsy-bitsy waist even after two pregnancies. The kids are wild and pretty off-the-wall, my son has real long hair clear down to his shoulders, he wants to be a musician, they've both got artistic talent, they're different than all the other kids, we're different than everybody else in general. I know you don't resent my sitting here and daydreaming. I'll make a rolled roast today, Werner can go ahead and eat till he bursts, can he ever put it away, when his plate's empty I load him up with seconds right away, I mean, it's not like we're poor. The hose on the washing machine is kaput, I'll have to get a new one, plumbers cost way too much, Werner should have taken up a skilled trade, those guys clean up nowadays. My Werner, the pipe dreamer, I'm the one who does all the worrying, I can add and subtract. Karin had to write a paper last week on Sisyphus, don't make me laugh, schlepping a stupid stone uphill, just let him keep this house for one week and his boulder would seem like a pebble. Maybe what gets him down is doing the same thing every day, just like me. But at least he's not weighed down with debts, except that when we finally do get to the top, we'll have our own home, and Sisyphus has zilch. I have to keep pushing Werner every day, keep him moving, one foot in front of the other. I keep you hid from him, my diary is nobody's business.*

Werner was barely out of the house when Carmen realized he had forgotten his satchel. She ran to the door, spotted the taillights of his car (not paid for yet, either), waved the satchel rather helplessly, thought about it for a moment, and rode off after him on her bike. She couldn't catch up with him, and so she cycled all the way to the factory on the far side of the small town.

Satchel under her arm, she walked through the plant while conveyor belts of toy pistols, tanks, robots and plastic soldiers rolled past her, but she couldn't find Werner anywhere. She went to the personnel office, gave old Frau Busch, the secretary, a friendly smile, asked for her husband, she was just bringing him his satchel, and Frau Busch looked back at her, in total, speechless surprise, until she finally managed to say: "Your husband? You mean you don't know?" Carmen shook her head, and Frau Busch choked on her next sentence as if on some indigestible lump: "He doesn't work here anymore, hasn't for two months now . . . Orders are way down . . . more than fifty people were let go . . . you didn't know?" Carmen was no longer listening, she turned silently and made her way back through the plant. She flinched as someone grabbed her shoulder from behind, Herr Fröhlich, the assistant director, all apologetic grimaces but not uttering a word, who finally reached for the conveyor belt and shoved into her hand two toy pistols that looked deceptively like the genuine article. "For your little boy and girl," he said. "They're not so little anymore," Carmen replied, lost in thought. "Take them, please. I'm really very sorry, but what can we do. Our spe-

cialty is war toys, after all, and orders have been . . .
this whole peace movement thing has played havoc
with us. We've got to rethink things, here, look at
this"—he pointed to small plastic men meant to look
like policemen, while down the belt next to them
little barbarians rolled—"those are the demonstra-
tors, and these are the police. The game'll be called
Battle at the Reactor, and if that doesn't sell, we can
close up shop . . ." Carmen left him standing there,
walked on, clutching the two pistols, which she finally
stuck in her purse once she was outside.

She pedaled slowly toward home, passed her bank,
stopped and went in. Her hands trembled as she held
the statement, and Herr Fuchs, the young, very good-
looking branch manager, shook his head regretfully.
"Much as we'd like to, we simply cannot extend you
any further credit. And with the payments on your
house and car due, I don't know how you'll manage
it either. . . ." Carmen gazed at him, tears in her eyes
now. "Help us, please." "My dear woman, what can
I do?" "He'll find work, real soon, we'll catch up on
it all again, I know we will. But what are we supposed
to live on in the meantime?" "You must realize, of
course, that in order to pay off twenty thousand marks
of debt, you have to be earning at least forty thousand
a year. My guess is that there's no way you can avoid

bankruptcy." Carmen stared mutely at him and, holding herself as erect as possible, walked out of the bank.

*So it's all been for nothing. Fourteen years of work, for nothing. It's made him old and fat, both of us, not just him, but with him I can see it happening every day, the way he sits there across from me and the meat on his bones just droops more and more, like it was dragging him down, and when all we really wanted was to move up. We always thought that once we'd paid off the mortgage, then . . . then everything would be alright, then we'd have it made. But that all the time we were getting older and older, we forgot that somehow. The older you get, the happier you ought to be, right? That's only logical. That's really the same thing the bank says, too. If you start paying in your five marks as a baby, at forty you're rich and happy, sitting in the yard with your family. I have to wash my hair. That wiseass at the bank, Herr Fuchs, had such a disgusted look on his face, giving me the once-over from head to foot. When do I have time to get my hair done, huh? I'm happy Werner didn't tell me, that way he at least had to try and pretend to be in a good mood, because if there's one thing I can't stand, it's gloom and doom.*

She tried several times that day to tell Werner that she knew, but she couldn't bring herself to do it, especially after a discussion about choosing a career erupted during dinner between Werner and Rainer, and Werner said: "The worst thing in life is to realize you're a loser because you've got no job. That's why a career is so important, so that nobody can stomp on you later on, because a man without a job is a zero." "You mean standing around in a factory for a hundred years like you? Doing the same thing over and over? Nah, no way," Rainer said, "no job at all is better than that . . ." Carmen barged in between them shouting: "Well, all the same, it keeps you two in your trendy threads and the latest hairdos!" Karin laughed: "Ma, why're you yelling all of a sudden? Would you rather have two grungy punk-rockers?" "Maybe I would," Carmen said very softly, and the whole family fell silent and looked at her in amazement.

*I sat all night by the window, and Herr Schirmer did it again. Werner doesn't know about it, he always sleeps like a log. I often sit at the window like that in the dark when I can't sleep for all the arithmetic in my head, and then sometimes I see Herr Schirmer slinking out of his house in his undershorts and creeping all bent over through the rose bed, ours I mean, our lot extends up against the next house, and every time my heart starts in pounding, and he runs past along the boxwood hedge and then stands in front of his own bedroom window, the light on inside. The first time I almost called the police, because I didn't know it was Herr Schirmer. There he stands,*

*and yesterday was cold, but he's always just in his undershorts,
the curtains aren't closed, I can see it all clearly. She undresses,
very slowly, doing little twists and turns, she's not all that
pretty either, too skinny for my taste, and then she's naked,
and sometimes takes hold of her breasts, Frau Schirmer does,
nothing special either, mine are bigger. Then she turns out
the light and Herr Schirmer slinks back into the house. What
a pig. Sometime I'm going to tell her, when I run into her
at the supermarket. What has she got that other women
haven't got? Last night, I'm a little ashamed of myself, I
went out into the garden then too, after everything was dark
over at the Schirmers', and he was back in the house, and I
stood there in my nightie at our window, but there was just
my Werner laying there in bed, and the moonlight was shining
on his fat face. My poor Werner. I just stood there and my
feet were cold, and I thought about what it would be like if
I'd just keep on walking, right through the development, just
keep going, with everybody asleep, even Herr Schirmer, the
pig, and nobody would notice.*

The next morning Carmen claimed Werner wasn't
looking at all well and should just stay home. She held
a hand to his brow and decided he had a little fever.
Werner looked at her for a long time and then said:
"Maybe you're right," and stayed in bed.

Carmen made him some soup, started crying in the
process, and her tears fell into the pot. The doorbell

rang, and before she could summon up any resistance, a woman in heavy makeup claiming to be a cosmetic consultant shoved her way into the house. She laid her metal briefcase on the kitchen table, unpacked countless jars of makeup quick as a wink, looked hard at Carmen and said: "You don't look good at all. Now just let me go to work. You'll feel like a new person afterwards." She ordered Carmen to sit down, and while she painted away at her face, kept up a stream of unbearably cheerful chatter. "The better you look, the better you feel. You'll be amazed at all your energy once you see an attractive woman opposite you in the mirror and not some frazzled housewife with problems. The undoable becomes doable. You'll see."

She teased and piled Carmen's hair up on her head, snapped on a pair of gigantic earclips, demanded that she put on something pretty before looking in the mirror. Carmen slipped into Karin's tiger coat, which, even though it was fake fur, always looked terribly chic on Karin, then the peppy cosmetic consultant took her by the hand and led her to the bathroom. It seemed to Carmen that although she certainly wasn't a new person, she did indeed look radically different, in a high-toned and elegant way, like the real mother of her children. She smiled, the cosmetic consultant nodded her satisfaction and in no time had sold her some lotions, beauty creams and hair dye, presented her with a hefty bill for over 250 marks and vanished with some good advice: Carmen should just take a walk through town with her new face, then she'd see how great it feels to look good.

Carmen's wallet was empty following this mugging, and so was the fridge. Werner was asleep, and when Carmen carefully pulled his wallet from the pocket of his jacket, she saw that he was flat broke, too. Carmen shook her head in disbelief, kept opening and closing the fridge door, as if by some miracle that would fill it up, rummaged in the deep-freeze, where all she found was some petrified sprigs of parsley, went to the cellar and found one can of fruit, raspberries.

*Dear Diary, I haven't looked like this for fifteen years, I have especially beautiful eyes, that's what the cosmetic consultant said, and I should accentuate them. She ended up accentuating everything on me that's worth accentuating, going on a diet wouldn't hurt me either, as if I didn't know that. The perfect moment, since we don't have anything left to eat. Like Africans. Only for them it's easier to believe, they don't have a deep-freeze, or car, or TV, or their own house like we do, it really is hard to believe. I could bawl, but our last penny went for my accentuated eyes, and it'd be pure waste to ruin*

*this lovely makeup now too, when I haven't looked this good
for fifteen years. Werner doesn't want to look at anything,
he's dead to the world.*

She took the bus into town, went to the butcher's,
snapped her purse open, stared at the two toy pistols,
she had forgotten all about them, snapped the purse
shut and said with a smile: "Oh—now I've done it,
I've forgotten my wallet! Could you put it on my bill
maybe?" The woman in the butcher shop gave her a
sharp look: "If I knew who you were, sure, but . . ."
"What?" Only slowly did it dawn on Carmen, "You
don't recognize me? I'm Frau Müller." The woman
nodded tentatively now. "When you came in, I
thought you looked a little like Frau Müller . . . that
new hairdo really changes you. But you look nice,
really, really. And of course I'll put it on your bill.
But do tell, have there been some big changes in your
life? I mean financial changes . . . because you look so
. . . so different than usual . . ." "Yes"—Carmen's
smile vanished—"you could say there have been some
dramatic changes in our finances." "Well then, con-
gratulations," the woman said and Carmen stumbled
out of the shop into the daylight. She put on her
sunglasses and walked slowly down the street. A few
businessmen turned to watch her, and Carmen's first
thought was that something was wrong, her zipper
open maybe or her hem hanging, but the men were

smiling, and then she remembered something that lay far in the past, and she smiled back and walked on, an inch or two taller. Until she came to her bank. She stopped short, looked through the windowpane. The bank was empty. She opened her purse, pulled out a handkerchief and blew her nose. The two pistols stared innocently up at her. She looked around, walked into the bank, straight to the window, aimed the pistol at the cashier, then at all the other employees, whose mouths were clapping open and shut, like fish. Not a word was spoken. Mutely the cashier began shoving the bills through the slot. "All of it," Carmen whispered, "I want all of it." She did not see Herr Fuchs coming, because he had slipped around behind her and suddenly laid a hand on her shoulder. Very softly he said: "Frau Müller, calm down, just calm down. Give me the pistol." She whirled around and thrust the pistol against his chest. She shook her head, knew she had to say something now, but what? She had seen it all on TV often enough. But what came next? "Tell . . . tell them all . . . ," she started to stammer, "tell them to sit down, now, to sit down on their hands, otherwise . . . otherwise I'll blow your head off." Herr Fuchs turned pale, and sure enough, ordered his employees to sit down. With one hand Carmen went on threatening Herr Fuchs, with the other she stuffed the money into her purse, into her coat pockets, into her décolletage. "And now you're coming with me. Tell the others I'll kill you if they call the police." "Please," Herr Fuchs said in a monotone, "please, please don't." "Sorry," Carmen replied and even managed a little smile. Herr Fuchs obediently ordered the employees not to call the police, because his life hung in the balance, and Carmen shoved him ahead of her with the gun, out of the bank and across the street to the bus stop. Not a bus in sight. "You're only making it worse for yourself. Let me go, please!" "You've got yourself to blame. Nobody else recognized me, only you." "I swear to you I won't say a thing. No matter what, we're insured. . . ." His voice was quavering. At that moment a police car pulled up to the bank. Carmen broke into a sweat, until now she hadn't wasted a second thinking about what she was doing, it was all like sleepwalking. "That's not my fault. I wasn't the one who called the police, you know. I'm still young. Please don't," Herr Fuchs whimpered. Did he really think she'd gun him down in cold blood? But what was she going to do with him? Maybe he believed her and this ridiculous toy pistol, but she didn't believe a word he said. The bus came, and, jamming the pistol into his ribs, she commanded him to climb aboard. The outraged driver refused the five-hundred-mark bill she had fished out of her purse, and Carmen asked Herr Fuchs if he couldn't maybe help out with some change. He could, and paid the two fares.

. . .

They stood pressed tightly together on the over-crowded bus, and Carmen whispered into Herr Fuchs's ear: "If you try any tricks . . ." Herr Fuchs nodded obediently. After a few minutes, however, he turned to an elderly man standing directly in front of him and said loudly: "This woman here is threatening me with a pistol. Help me." Sweat beaded on Carmen's forehead, and she gave the old man a feeble smile. He grinned and said: "Well, the lady wouldn't have to threaten me with a pistol, I'd be happy to volunteer." The people standing nearby laughed. The bus made its stop in her neighborhood, Carmen shoved Herr Fuchs out of the bus and onto the street ahead of her. Wrapped around each other like lovers, they approached her house. "Could you maybe find another spot for that pistol? It's already bored a hole in me," Herr Fuchs said. "You know, the longer you keep this up, the longer you're going to be behind bars." "Keep your mouth shut and worry about staying healthy," Carmen replied gruffly, unlocked the door, pushed Herr Fuchs into the bathroom, bound him to the shower with adhesive tape and locked the door behind her.

*He smells good, uses some expensive after-shave. I had to press up against him because of the pistol. I haven't pressed up against another man since I got married, but that didn't hit me until I was standing beside him in the bus and I smelled him, he's got a handsome chin, real nice and chiseled, not like Werner's, he almost doesn't have one anymore, he's all neck, but a jutting masculine chin like that, clean shaven, I've got no use at all for beards, I sure would have loved to take hold of that chin right there above me. I'm only telling you what I was thinking. I know I ought to be trembling in my boots, for heaven's sake, I've just robbed a bank and tied up Herr Fuchs in the bathroom, but it's not like that, I wouldn't have taken him with me if he hadn't been so damn good-looking. Just like there always used to be one guy at every party or in dancing class, the one I never got, who never gave me so much as a glance, they all looked alike, handsomer than they had any right to be, but at some point I caught on that they were never going to look at pudgy little Carmen Cordes, and then along came Werner, handsome he wasn't, but striking. Back then. And on the way home he loaned me his gloves right off, and that convinced me. I really ought to tell him that.*

Werner was still asleep. Carmen awakened him gently with a kiss. He sat up in bed, stared at her. "My God, what have you done to yourself?"

"Werner, listen to me. I just robbed VG Bank and have taken Herr Fuchs hostage. He's in the bathroom." "Carmen, please. What's with that idiotic hairdo?" Carmen removed the hairpins, and her hair fell back into its usual shape. "Werner! Did you hear what I said?" "Yes," Werner said with a sleepy smile, "you just robbed VG Bank and Herr Fuchs is in the bathroom. Take off those awful earrings, please. They're not for you." Obediently, Carmen took off the earrings.

At that moment a yowling scream erupted. Carmen ran to the bathroom, fumbled awhile with the key. Werner, his face white, followed slowly behind her. The door opened, and there in the shower stood Herr Fuchs, soaking wet and shivering. In an attempt to untie himself he had hit the faucet. "Please turn the water off. It's cold as ice," Herr Fuchs said. Carmen turned off the shower, and at once Herr Fuchs began to yell for help. Without a second thought, Carmen stuffed a washcloth gag into his mouth. "Do you believe me now?" she said to Werner. He nodded, speechless. Carmen pulled money from her coat pockets, from her décolletage, held her purse out to him without comment. A smile of bliss passed across Werner's face. He burrowed his hands in the money, tossed it into the air. "What are we going to do with him?" Carmen cocked her head at Herr Fuchs, who was shaking in misery. "Did anybody recognize you?" Werner asked, suddenly sobered. "Only him. That's why he's here. I had to take him with me." Carmen plugged in a hair dryer. "Here. Blow him dry. The kids'll be home soon." "What are we going to tell them?" Werner was slowly catching on, and panic took hold. Carmen silently thrust the hair dryer into his hand, and Werner obediently aimed it at Herr Fuchs.

*I've got no illusions about this, I'm too old for that. He only came along because of the pistol. All the same, there was a look of respect in his eyes for that attractive woman I was this morning. Werner didn't like it at all, naturally, he doesn't like changes of any kind, which is why I can't dye my hair, something I'd really like to do sometime, he'd just give me silent, disapproving looks until I finally went back to my mousy-gray all on my own. It wasn't just Herr Fuchs who looked at me different today, they all expected me to give the orders, wanted to obey me, because as a rule good-looking people get their way, it wasn't just the pistol, I'm sure it wasn't. And it wasn't really Carmen Müller who robbed the bank either. Now that I've combed out my hair, washed off the makeup, my heart's started pounding. The schnitzel's done. Here are the kids.*

They sat at their midday meal. "But I've got to go to the john. Can't we break down the door?" Rainer said. "A locksmith. Let's call a locksmith, I need my makeup." "I'm sure I'll find the bathroom key again," Carmen said and forced a smile. "And if you've got to go to the bathroom, then go over to the Schirmers'." "We can't ring the Schirmers' doorbell and say, excuse us, we've got to pee-pee, because in a fit of mental derangement our mother locked the door to the toilet and threw away the key." "I am capable of some other things, too," Carmen said calmly, "in my fits of mental derangement as you call it. . . ." Karin and Rainer fell silent and looked worriedly at their mother. Carmen got up and cleared the table. Rainer turned on the radio, the news. An announcer was saying: ". . . robbed today by a well-dressed woman. She is approximately five feet three inches tall, wore her hair up, had on dark sunglasses and a striped tiger coat. She got away with thirty thousand marks and took the branch manager hostage. She managed to escape with him. If you have any information . . ." Carmen and Werner stared anxiously at each other. Rainer looked for a station with music, Karin said contemptuously, "Everybody's wearing tiger coats now, I don't even like mine anymore." And Rainer commented: "For thirty thousand marks, how can anyone be that dense? Any fool knows you can't make anything off of banks." Carmen went on washing up. "Have you got any plans for this afternoon?" she asked Karin and Rainer. "Nah, why?" Carmen and Werner traded a quick glance, then Carmen reached for her purse, pulled out a five-hundred-mark bill, gave it to the kids and said: "Okay, divide it between you and you can each buy whatever you want. And I mean right now. Pop and I have something we have to discuss." Rainer and Karin hesitated for a moment, looked worriedly at their parents, but then ambled off. They were barely out the door when Werner said: "And what if the bills are numbered?"

Carmen took the gag out of Herr Fuchs's mouth, brandished the pistol at him and asked if the bills were numbered. "Please, untie me." He sounded miserable. "Only if you tell us if the bills are numbered." He said they weren't, Carmen apologized, stuck the washcloth back in his mouth and closed the door. "I feel sorry for him," Werner said. "Me, too," Carmen replied, "but we can't just let him go." To her surprise, she started to cry. Werner hugged her. Tears were in his eyes as well. "If only you'd told me you'd lost your job ..." she sobbed. "I couldn't. I felt so ashamed." "But you don't have to feel ashamed with me." "I felt ashamed in front of the kids. . . ." Carmen was hugging him now. "Werner, I have to leave. Disappear. Into the underground, I think that's what they call it. You haven't done anything. But I have." "I'm coming with you," Werner said with determination. Carmen was against this, it wasn't for him, but when he insisted and said: "I won't leave you alone," it touched her.

Carmen couldn't decide what she should pack for "the underground." She stood there in front of her closet. Summer things? Winter things? Rubber boots? Heels? "Werner, do you think we should take our swimsuits?" "We're not going on vacation, Carmen!" "Well, you never know."

Carmen left a letter for the kids, in which she claimed that Werner's health demanded he go somewhere for treatment, she was accompanying him, they would definitely be back soon, the money she was enclosing was for food, and they were to go right on attending school as always, please.

They put their bags and Herr Fuchs, bundled up with clothesline like a package, into the car and drove off. After a few hundred yards, Carmen remembered she had forgotten her curling iron, and underground or no, she wasn't about to run around like some slut. Werner groaned, but drove back, and Carmen went into the house, returning with both curling iron and a thick folder. "Okay," she ordered, "now we're going to drive to VG Bank and pay off our debts. You go in there, these are our bills, and write out the checks. Then go over to the cashier and deposit the cash." She carefully arranged the money in her purse into a neat bundle. "But I can't just go in there and redeposit the same money you just stole," Werner said lamely.

"If we don't pay off these latest warnings, in a couple of days the court'll sic the bailiff on the kids. Is that what you want?" "I can't," Werner said, "I'm afraid."

Carmen reminded him to hit the door-lock switch so Herr Fuchs couldn't just climb out. She sat in the backseat with her hostage and threw a blanket over them both. Werner, knees trembling, went into the bank.

Two policemen were standing at the entrance. The teller whom Carmen had threatened a few hours ago was so despondent that he didn't even look up when Werner laid 28,000 marks in the tray and said with a quavering voice that he would like to deposit the money in his account.

Under the blanket, Carmen asked Herr Fuchs if he had a family, and when he shook his head she said that she was glad, because she already had a very bad conscience in any case, not on account of the robbery, in fact the bank now had its money back, except for two thousand marks, but her kids had to eat, right? But she was really sorry, very sorry, for him. This wasn't at all like her, you see, and as for Werner, why he was the salt of the earth, he'd see that soon enough. Werner returned. He was shaking like an aspen leaf and almost plowed into the car ahead of him.

Once they were out of town, they started arguing. Carmen wanted to head south, Werner was for north. "Herr Fuchs should decide," Carmen demanded he give thumbs down for south, up for north. Herr Fuchs preferred the south, too. They pulled onto the autobahn and headed for Munich.

"C'mon, Werner, let's see you laugh," Carmen said, "the weather's beautiful, we're headed south, let's see you laugh." "My wife has robbed a bank, we've got a hostage in the backseat, it's no laughing matter." "Oh, pooh," Carmen said, in a good mood now.

They had to get gas, and it turned out that except for twenty marks, they had no money left, which Carmen justified by saying that, after all, she had wanted to take as little money as possible from the bank, and that they had really only "moved it around" a little. "Do you think that makes things any better, 'moving it around'? Bank robbery is bank robbery, and now we still don't have enough money to get gas." "But hardly any debts. What do you want, Werner? You can't have everything. Maybe he's got . . . ?" She turned around to Herr Fuchs, apologizing before she pulled his wallet out of his pocket. Not bad, he had almost five hundred marks on him plus a couple of credit cards. "We'll pay it all back," Carmen promised.

*Werner's pumping gas, I don't have much time, he'll be right back. Do you remember Sisyphus? I just dropped the damn stone, it's still rolling down the mountain. Werner doesn't understand, he says I've only made things worse. He was determined to come along, to protect me. But my question is, who's protecting who here, but he is sweet when he says, Carmen, I'll protect you. Herr Fuchs is single. I asked. It's a shame we have to keep him tied up, that's really the only thing that bothers me, that he's not here of his own free will. Werner is worried about me, he thinks I'm in shock and that's why I'm in such a good mood. I've got to get myself under control, because I could just shout for joy, everything has changed all of a sudden, from minute to minute nothing is predictable anymore, as if I had made a date with a total stranger. A while ago, just for a moment, I lost my courage and thought this can only come to a terrible end, but now that we're on the road I feel like my uneasiness has just been whisked away, and I know that we really have no way at all of influencing whatever is going to happen. I'm not to blame anymore, do you understand what I mean? Like I've been told to 'get out of town' and I'm out.*

It grew dark, and Werner grew weary. They drove off the autobahn into the nearest large town. Carmen waved Herr Fuchs's credit cards. "I've always wanted to stay in some swanky hotel." "But what are we going to do with him?" "We take him along." "The police are sure to have put out a bulletin with his description long ago. And besides, we'll have a hard time leading him through the lobby all tied up," Werner said. "You always think of everything." Carmen gazed at her husband in admiration. The bellboy almost collapsed under the weight of their suitcase and dragged it, inch by inch, to the elevator. "May I ask what you have in there?" Carmen tossed him a friendly glance and said: "Our two children. We always carry them around that way." The bellboy gave an agonized smile.

He set the suitcase in the room, turned on all the lights, showed them how to operate the TV and the minibar. Carmen and Werner stared spellbound at the suitcase, which now began to move, lurching back and forth, until it finally toppled over with a loud thud. The bellboy winced, set it upright again and fled the room.

Carmen ordered something to eat from room service. Herr Fuchs sat tied in a chair, a lump of misery. "Werner, take that washcloth out of his mouth and ask him what he wants." The gag was barely out of Herr Fuchs's mouth, when he started to shout loudly for help. Werner stood there paralyzed, Fuchs screamed as if he'd been skewered. In the next room someone pounded on the wall and bellowed: "Turn down the TV." Carmen made a plucky grab for the nape of Herr Fuchs's neck and stuffed the rag back in his mouth. From next door came a loud thank-you.

Exhausted, Werner and Carmen sank onto the bed. Fuchs was gagging on his washcloth. "I can't watch that any longer," said Carmen. "I wish I'd blown his brains out right then and there." "Carmen, how can you say a thing like that?" "That's what they always say on TV. It's funny, when you've got a gun in your hand like that, and suddenly everybody does what you tell them because you've got it, you can really acquire a taste for it. . . ." She twirled the toy pistol the way they do in westerns and whispered into Werner's ear: "We've got to intimidate him."

Herr Fuchs was gagging on the washcloth so disgustingly that Werner could stand it no longer. He took Carmen's pistol away, held it to Herr Fuchs's temple and removed the washcloth from his mouth. "Okay," he said, "one more scream and you've had it." "Oh, I won't. I promise. I have to go to the toilet." Werner looked helplessly at Carmen, but she was pointing at him. "No sir, I'm not going to hold his . . . his thing, too," Werner said. "Maybe I should, huh?" Carmen had to giggle. "If we tie his hands in front of him, he can do it himself. . . ." "Excuse me for interfering, but how would it be if you untie me, I go to the toilet, and then you tie me up again." "I

don't know," Werner said. "I don't trust him."
"Please, I'm going to pee my pants," Herr Fuchs
begged. "We take no risks," Carmen decided and she
accompanied him to the john, unzipped his zipper,
turned around and with her eyes closed stuck out her
hand. "This is too embarrassing. I can't do it," Herr
Fuchs said. "Don't make such a fuss. I have a son,"
Carmen replied coolly. After that, he could, and Carmen felt hurt.

*I've locked myself in the bathroom. Werner and Herr Fuchs
are talking now, he took the gag out of his mouth, I'm very
glad about that, he looked so ugly with it in. Werner can't
stand him, but he realizes we can't just let him go. My God,
he is good-looking, and I don't mean just his face, let me
tell you. I could very well have carried on with him, alone
in the toilet, and him tied up, completely helpless. It would
never enter Werner's mind, he can't imagine I'd do such a
thing. I really had to get hold of myself, otherwise I would
have fondled him, I think he even expected me to, but I'm
not a pervert, not with a man who's all tied up. I don't feel
sorry for him, nobody feels sorry for beautiful people, only
them for us, there's fat Herr Müller and his short, ugly wife,
I can tell how sorry they feel for us, all those beautiful,
successful people, they always smile that sweet smile. I'm glad
my hostage is so beautiful, and doesn't look like the two of
us, because then I'd feel sorry for him, and it would be no
fun at all. I'd love to untie Herr Fuchs, and then make him*

*undress and sit down naked on the bed. All I'd do is just*
*stare at him and enjoy the view. Werner has absolutely no*
*fantasy for something like that.*

Together they drank the minibar empty, and Herr
Fuchs was getting obviously drunk. "Shouldn't we be
on a first-name basis," he suggested, "if we're all three
going to be lying in a double bed together?" His name
was Lothar. They toasted the occasion, and Carmen
made the charming remark that she was happy to
have taken such a relatively nice hostage. At the bank
he had always seemed so terribly arrogant. "Do you
know," Lothar said, "what I simply cannot get over?
How can anyone rob a bank where she's a customer
herself?" "Because the woman at the butcher shop
didn't recognize me . . . and I've known her for a
couple of years now. . . ." "Werner," Lothar said and
gave him a nudge, "you've got a crazy woman for a
wife, you know that?" "I'd forgotten," Werner replied, "but actually she was always like that. She
waylaid me fourteen years ago. Back when I was still
trim and handsome, too." "Now don't go getting any
fancy ideas, Lothar"—Carmen gave him a poke in
the side—"you're not here because of your alabaster
body."

"You know"—Lothar clapped his mouth open and
let Carmen pour whiskey down his throat—"what
I'd really like? If I could hold my own glass and not

have to suck on a bottle like a baby. It's humiliating to have a woman pour your whisky down you. A real man does his own drinking. I'm really much too drunk to pull any tricks." Carmen stood up, swaying, locked the door to the room and hid the key behind the toilet. "Untie him, Werner," she said. "No reason for him to live like a dog, either."

Lothar rubbed his raw wrists, grinned broadly at them both, suddenly dived forward and in his hand was the pistol that Carmen had laid on top of the TV. "Okay," Lothar said coolly and suddenly very sober, "you're both really very nice, but also as dim-witted as they come. Now just lie down on your tummies real pretty and extend your arms. C'mon, c'mon, what's taking so long?" Werner, drunk and frightened, promptly accommodated by turning over on his stomach. Lothar sat down atop his rear end and held the pistol to Carmen's temple. "And now you're going to tie up your hero husband, otherwise there's going to be an ugly hole in that pretty head, Carmencita." Carmen gave Lothar a look of fury, hauled her arm way back and punched him in the face. In his amazement, he dropped the pistol, Carmen grabbed it, pointed it at him, and Lothar promptly put both hands in the air. "Forgive me," he said, "I didn't mean it the way it looked. Carmen, please." "Frau Müller to you. On your knees!" Lothar knelt beside the bed, his hands still raised, Werner slowly turned over. "The way you pull it off, sweetheart . . ." he said softly.

Lothar Fuchs was lying tied up in bed, snoring, Carmen was pacing the room, Werner couldn't sleep, either. "I could kill him for that now, I really could. If you were a snorer I would have divorced you long ago," Carmen said. She played with the pistol, pulled the second one from her purse, drew from the hip like an old-time cowboy. "And to think he fell for these things . . ." "They don't look so genuine anymore, not the way the prototype did. We weren't allowed to ship any of them for just that reason, that's what ruined the company. That's why they let me go. They couldn't cover their losses any other way," Werner said. "And us? How are we supposed to 'cover' ours? And because of a couple of lousy toy pistols I had to go rob a bank, just so we didn't end up in a shelter for the homeless?" "Or in jail," Werner said dryly. "Which is where we already are. With him around it's like being in jail. We've got him on our backs now for good, and he's getting on my nerves! We can't carry him around town in a suitcase forever. The moment he's recognized, it's all over. It's all over, anyway. Let's not kid ourselves. We would have managed somehow on unemployment. . . ." "Oh yeah?" Carmen said caustically. "I'd like to see you explain to our kids that they have to wear the same clothes for the next three years. And the house. We dreamed about that for ten years. Can you imagine what it would feel like to move out of our house and into three rooms in public housing?" "We're three to a room right now, and he's not even part of the family," said Werner bitterly.

*It always ends with them snoring and reading the paper over breakfast. No matter how pretty you've pictured it all to yourself at the start, that's how it ends. Werner has gone for a walk. Lothar is snoring and looks like he's having sweet dreams too, he wears such a funny grin when he sleeps, maybe he's sitting under palm trees with some naked blonde. He would have shot us in cold blood if he could have. And I still help him pee. He isn't the least bit interested in me, for him we're just idiots, always were. He despises us. I could hold a pillow over his face until he stops snoring, stops breathing. I bet he'd be very surprised if an idiot like me killed him, Lothar Fuchs, branch manager for VG Bank. He'd be pretty teed off for it to be someone like me, of all people. A while ago I laid down next to him for a minute, real close. I don't want anything from him, really, I just wanted to try out how it feels when the guy you've always sort of imagined is actually laying next to you. And when you're beside him, do you then imagine somebody else too? I know Werner doesn't, he's got way too little imagination for that. I just wanted to snuggle up to him a little, what's the harm in that, but he just grunted, our Herr Fuchs, and rolled over.*

. . .

"He's got to look different!" Carmen rummaged in her cosmetic case and proudly pulled out a package of hair dye, platinum blond. "That cosmetic consultant talked me into this stuff, for my gray hair."

Werner held the sleeping, and snoring, Lothar in his arms, while Carmen lathered his brown hair with hydrogen peroxide. "Let's hope the stink doesn't wake him up," she whispered.

Even the sumptuous champagne breakfast that Carmen ordered from room service could not console Lothar. He lay there mute and bound in the bed and wouldn't respond, wouldn't eat anything, wouldn't drink anything. With the patience of an angel, Carmen tried talking to him, but nothing helped. "Don't you see, Lothar," Werner said, "we had to do it," and he held the newspaper that had come with breakfast under his nose. The headline read: WOMAN BANK ROBBER VANISHES WITH HOSTAGE. Under it an artist's sketch of Carmen, which didn't look at all like her, and a photograph of Lothar Fuchs, which looked very like him before the dye job. "He's depressed," Werner said. "I know what it's like. That's how I've felt for the last two months." "Look, he's crying," Carmen bent down to Lothar. Silent tears ran down his face. She patted his brow and gave him a kiss. She looked apologetically at Werner. He shrugged. Carmen began reading the newspaper report for Lothar. The word "heavyset" in their description of her infuriated her, but when she got to the last sentence, "No demands have been made thus far," Lothar came to life. He sat up, wiped the tears from his face. "Demands," he said slowly. "Why haven't you made any demands?" "What sort of demands?" Carmen and Werner asked, flabbergasted. "Money, of course." "Yes, money . . . ," Carmen echoed. "We could demand ransom for you. How much? What do you think, Lothar?" "Bullshit," Werner objected, "I've seen it all on TV, they always nab you when the money gets passed." "We'll split it fifty-fifty, and I'll be silent as a tomb." Lothar was suddenly very alert. "If you think you've got debts, then you should see mine. Not with VG Bank, of course. Nowadays it's total idiocy not to have debts, it all gets eaten up by taxes otherwise. . . ."

"How much would you say you're worth?" Carmen asked the practical question. "Well let's see . . . about half a million for sure." "Two hundred fifty thousand for us, Werner!" Carmen's face grew radiant. "Count me out, they're not going to waste half a million on a guy like this. And even if they would, you can never touch the money again. . . ." "He's right," Lothar said and was about to fall back into his depression, but right before he did, an idea apparently struck him. His voice heavy with import, he said: "If you two will trust me, I'll make all three of us rich. You just have to trust me. I have a brilliant idea."

*He looks pretty silly with his blond hair, like a gigolo. I have forgiven him. He has a brilliant idea, but won't let us in on it. Werner doesn't trust him one inch, he's driving me crazy he's so suspicious. He wants to go home, to the kids. I don't. Werner says I'm heartless. Maybe I am. I lost my heart cleaning house, they all let it shrivel up, Werner and the kids did, with the mess they left behind every day, and never a word of recognition when it had disappeared again in the evening, as if by a miracle. The miracle was me, the silent miracle, like miracles always are. Werner insists that he knows what's ahead. The police and prison. When he must know that you can never know what's ahead. You're always just sort of groping along. Sometimes it's like I'm looking through a kaleidoscope, I shake it back and forth, but it just won't turn out right. I keep thinking if I can only shake it enough, it'll disappear, but all I get is some new pattern that still isn't the right one, but one that we have to stick with. I'm glad that Lothar has had a brilliant idea, and I don't even want him to let us in on it, he has to decide what happens now, and I'll follow the way a loyal wife should. In my own mind, I've married him, that's less of an effort, makes him far less attractive, I simply have two husbands now. Not bad.*

Lothar was kneeling before Carmen and Werner, he was tied to the bedpost by one hand and the other was raised for the oath. Carmen said: "I will never betray Carmen and Werner Müller to the police, I swear by . . . by my own life." Lothar repeated it after her. Carmen went on: "I will divide the money, down to the pfennig, with Carmen and Werner Müller . . ." "Fifty-fifty," Lothar interjected. "Why don't we just divide it in thirds?" Carmen asked. "Not gonna amount to anything anyway," Werner said wearily. He threw himself on the bed. "You're always so negative." Carmen untied Lothar. "He's sworn an oath, after all."

"First of all, we need cash, they'll pick up our trail right off if we use credit cards." Lothar was once again the dynamic young man he'd been before being taken prisoner. He took both pistols in his hand: "And we get our cash with a gun."

"Those aren't real pistols at all," Carmen said with a grin. Lothar turned pale. "And I fell for that?" "They're the reason I lost my job . . . ," Werner said laconically.

Lothar called it "the overload system." By which he meant that if you robbed as many banks as possible in the shortest space of time, the police would be overloaded. He found three rural VG Banks, all very close to one another, he got the names of the towns from a little brochure that he carried in his wallet. "Around eleven is the best time. The dead space.

That's when banks are emptiest, only the retirees come in. I'll drive, and Carmen'll withdraw the money."

It was hard to get Werner excited about the idea, but Carmen explained to him that there was no difference between the punishment for one bank robbery and that for four, and besides they could be glad Lothar was no longer their hostage.

The first village had a drowsy, deserted look. A short, stooped old woman on a cane was walking across the marketplace toward the bank. Except for two tellers, who hardly looked up as the woman entered, the bank was empty. Beneath her hat, pulled down low over her face, the old woman wore sunglasses. She walked up to the cashier, poked around in her purse, pulled out a pistol, which she then aimed at the teller, and a memo pad, on which was written: "Hand over the money." She flipped the page, now it read: "Or you're dead," and on the next page, "Be quick about it." The teller did not hesitate long.

Moving ponderously on her cane, the old woman came out of the bank, only to make a very agile run for a green Ford rolling slowing toward her. The tires squealed, the car shot off.

In the next town, a very short man in a suit much too large for him and with a fedora on his head entered the bank, pulled a gun from his jacket and said in a deep voice: "This is a stickup." Only then did the man notice that there wasn't a soul in the bank. And only in response to his loud "hello" did a teller finally emerge from the toilet and appear behind his window, and then the man repeated what he had said.

At the third bank, a woman entered wearing an elegant dress that reached to her ankles, a turban and tinted glasses. She took a lipstick from her tiny handbag and a pistol from her bodice. She used the lipstick to write STICK UP across the teller's glass window, which the teller, who happened to be wearing thick glasses, had trouble deciphering at first. And while he worked himself into a fury over what this lady thought she was doing smearing up his bank and appeared to take no notice whatever of the pistol, the lady tried again and wrote it backwards for him on the glass. That shut him up, and he shoved the money through the slot in a hurry.

Carmen sat in the back seat in the midst of a mountain of old clothes and counted the money. Her tally was 21,000 marks and she beamed. "Three banks in twenty-six minutes. That's a record, don't you think?" "My girl, you were first-class," Lothar said. Werner was silent. "At least give me a kiss." Carmen held her cheek out to him. Werner didn't give her one.

"What's become of us?" he said gloomily. "And what were we before all this?" Carmen asked, taking offense. "Law-abiding citizens," Werner said. "Right, and we would have gone on being law-abiding citizens if they would have let us. . . ." Carmen was deeply disappointed by Werner's reaction. "Nobody forced us to rob banks!" Werner shouted, and he hadn't done that for a long time. "It's nerves," Lothar said, "he's afraid for you." Carmen hugged Werner and covered his face with kisses. Lothar looked at them, shaking his head with a trace of envy. "We've got to ditch this car," he said, all business now, "and get ourselves another one."

They drove on in silence until they came to a display lot for RV's and campers. At which point Werner said softly: "Am I allowed to wish for something, too? I've always wanted a camper . . . for the whole family . . ."

The dealer sat in his office reading a porn mag as a gigantic RV rolled slowly off his lot. A dachshund lying at his feet in its basket sprang up barking like crazy. "Shut up, Lumpi, and don't bother me," said the dealer and kissed his playmate of the month.

The "acquisition" of the RV, as Lothar elegantly put it, had convinced Werner, his mood improved. "If only the kids could be here," he repeated several times. Which reminded Carmen that she had to call home. They stopped at a phone booth, and while Carmen made her call, Lothar said to Werner: "I'll bet you've never been unfaithful to Carmen, right?" Werner shook his head. "I envy you two," Lothar continued, "people like you don't really exist. But you're going to have to be unfaithful to her. Just once. And for a great deal of money." Werner looked at him dumbfounded and did not understand.

Carmen was disappointed. "The kids aren't missing us much. They've already thrown three parties, and I wouldn't want to see what the house looks like . . . have a good relaxing vacation, they said." There were tears in Carmen's eyes. "How would it be if we spend a little money, huh?" Lothar asked, trying to comfort Carmen. "I was thinking for example of a fur coat." Carmen stopped crying.

In a department store they decked themselves out in brand-spanking new wardrobes. Carmen got her fur coat, Lothar and Werner treated themselves to sinfully expensive new suits. "Crime has to pay," Lothar said and talked Werner into a whole stack of silk shirts. It was fun to see the Müllers happy, and he was amazed at their transformation.

.  .  .

*Dressed to kill, that's my Werner, and he's gotten thinner too. It's the fear, he says, that makes him thinner. Even though he's not nearly as scared now that we have our camper. He's so proud of it, this morning he washed and waxed it. I would love to have a picture of us both, me in my fur and Werner in his new suit, he looks like some big shot in it. To think you can change so much just with money, simply make yourself different whenever you feel like it. I'm sitting here in my fur coat on the couch in our camper, putting on my lipstick, I am Carmen Müller, the bank robber. It's different for Lothar, he always looks classy, no matter what he has on. I'd like to know how he does that. It's not his good looks, he's not all that good-looking anymore, when he eats he chews so funny, I can't even watch him, he has a way of using the world, it's at his beck and call, he just has to whistle and everybody jumps. If we ever tried whistling, they'd just toss us out. There are people who go to a restaurant and simply send the schnitzel back if it's too salty, and the waiters are still friendly. We eat it, and the waiters despise us. I don't know why, either, I can rob banks okay, but I can't send my food back.*

They spent the night at a camping ground, sat compatibly outside the RV drinking beer, eating sauerbraten that Carmen had made, and Lothar passed around a photograph of a bespectacled blonde in her early thirties. "She's a little inhibited," he explained, "that's why it never worked out with us. But a top-notch programmer. She designed the entire software program for VG Bank. Once during . . . mmmyes, during the transports of love, she told me how she's built a secret code word into all her programs, a kind of signature. And using this code word she can get back into her programs any time she likes." "So what?" Carmen and Werner asked, not understanding. "She would never tell it to me . . . but maybe to you, Werner . . . She likes fat men."

Lothar was snoring away below them in the RV, Carmen and Werner were whispering softly. "Werner, honey, don't make such a fuss. Think of all that money." "I haven't seduced a woman for twenty-five years, and if I'm gonna do it, I'll pick her out myself." "She looks like a pretty good number to me," Carmen said. "You sound like a pimp," Werner said in shock. "If I can rob four banks, you can at least swipe a code word." "She'll just turn on her heels and head the other way when she sees me." "Well that'd only prove she's got no taste in men period." Werner was not convinced.

*I wouldn't tell anyone but you, but we haven't done it for years. Werner is my best friend, and who goes to bed with their best friend? Closing your eyes doesn't help at all, maybe it takes a little bit of hate to do it, but how am I supposed to hate him, I know him too well. He gets on my nerves often enough, but that's not the same thing. If I could think, you rotten beast you, I'm going to turn you into mush, pure mush, till you don't even know who you are, you're at my mercy, like a baby, and afterwards you can be a rotten beast again, but right now, now I've got you, sort of like that. The way it was at the beginning, when we were still strangers. So let him have a go with this programmer person, then I could hate him a little, and maybe it would be like it used to be again.*

They drove into the city where Gabriele Gessmann, the programmer, lived, parked the RV in front of her place, and waited. Carmen cut out newspaper articles about the incredible bank robberies and the missing hostage, Lothar Fuchs. She couldn't help feeling a certain pride.

Lothar told Werner all the essentials about Gabriele Gessmann and even started to wax a little rapturous about her. "Why don't you go ahead and do it yourself?" Werner asked grumpily. "Because a woman would never do a favor for a man who never called again afterwards."

She came down the street, plastic bags in both hands. "Hey, she's a lot prettier than in the picture," said Carmen and looked wistfully at her Werner. Lothar gave the signal, both men climbed out. Lothar ran straight for Gabriele and simply upended her.

Werner walked slowly toward her, helped her gather up the groceries that had rolled out of the bags, and they walked together into the house.

Using the other side of the street, Lothar came back to the RV. "He's pulled it off," Carmen said. "Just like that. My Werner just picked up a woman." "Knocks your socks off, huh?" Lothar asked. "Sometimes I think you two are really weird. Married this long and never an affair . . ." "Don't think I haven't dreamed of it sometimes either . . . but it's enough to dream about it. It's usually better than the real thing, anyway." "You think so?" Lothar asked. "May I kiss you?" Carmen looked at him in astonishment. "If we divide it in thirds, sure." "Agreed," Lothar said and kissed Carmen.

Werner was sitting on the couch with Gabriele, drinking cognac and playing a computer game with her. "You've got to fire, keep firing," she shouted excitedly. "I haven't got a chance against you," Werner said, "not against a pro." "Yes, it's the only thing I do well." Gabriele fell unexpectedly into profound gloom. "Almost every day I drive to a different town, program, come back in the evening, sit here alone and play computer games. A pretty boring life, huh?" She started to cry. Werner helplessly laid a hand on her shoulder.

. . .

Lothar was lying in the RV's double bed with Carmen and kissing her. "Oh, come on," he said, "you did promise me, you know." "I have cellulite and pregnancy stretch-marks." "Doesn't matter." "But it does to me. And besides, I'd just be thinking of Werner the whole time." Lothar sat up with a groan and buttoned up his shirt.

"Oh God," he said, "sometimes I really hate you both. You're not good-looking, you're not successful, but you're so damned happy. What am I doing wrong?" "Maybe you want too much," Carmen noted cautiously. "Yes, I want it all. You two, you're so gruesomely modest, robbing a bank to pay your bills! Ha! I want it all, do you hear?" And after a pause: "And I wish just once somebody'd love me."

He started to cry. Carmen took him in her arms, comforted him the way she would a child, and said: "But for that you've got to love somebody first. You were a real bastard at the bank. People like us, you never gave a shit about them. Turned down our loan like a cold-blooded snake, but of course gave the millionaires theirs. Because we were unimportant to your career. You're cold-blooded, Lothar." He sobbed in her lap: "But in my job you have to be, otherwise you can just hang it up." "But is it worth it?" Carmen asked, which only led to renewed sobbing from Lothar.

. . .

Gabriele and Werner were a little drunk by now. "Please, please tell me your secret," Gabriele said tipsily. "Only if you won't cry anymore," Werner responded, and Gabriele threw herself on his chest, smiled at him and said: "I promise."

In the meantime Carmen and Lothar had taken up a game of Scrabble. Carmen was close to winning. Lothar laid down SEX, grinned at Carmen and said: "You miss the simplest opportunities." "We're having fun all the same, aren't we?" Lothar kissed her forehead. "You're the most fantastic woman I've ever met in my life," he said. Carmen looked out the window to hide her emotions—and let out a soft cry. Werner was heading directly for the RV, with Gabriele.

"I told her everything," Werner said, "she's in." Lothar looked as if he were going to faint. Gabriele smiled at him and said: "You're not bad as a blond, either." Lothar stammered: "I'm sorry I never called you that time." Silence. Until Werner started to laugh.

*Naturally she's tall and slim and beautiful. Werner reeks of her. I could strangle him. He just laughs. He's so totally changed, sits there grinning away, so damned sure of himself. But I couldn't do it with Lothar. Suddenly he actually nauseated me. If I talk about money maybe he'll stop, I thought, but that only turned him on, whispered in my ear about all those millions we'd have soon, is that perverted or what, I ask you? I could picture every detail, his hands creeping up and up, then massaging away at my breasts and panting, all pretty tacky, I didn't want to see him like that, like a frog squatting there on top of me. He cut it out quick enough, real quick, like a kid that's lost interest in a toy, nobody's going to treat me like that. And then he cried, he was so small and ugly all of a sudden, I wiped his nose for him, he was so unhappy. I like that, seeing princes get depressed, it's simply not fair, and then I tried to cheer him up so that he'd stop crying and turn handsome again, like he's supposed to be. Now we've got a princess besides, skin as white as snow, how in the hell did Werner manage it, I hate him for it. He just laughs.*

They sat in Gabriele's apartment at the computer, and Gabriele hammered around on the keyboard. "Okay, now here comes the code word for the VG banks," she said. On the screen two words appeared: DARLING LOTHAR. "That's the code word?" Lothar asked, thunderstruck. "I was pretty smitten with you at the time," Gabriele replied shyly, only to take charge of the action again, suddenly cool as a commander-in-chief. "Here we have all the people with accounts in VG banks. Our best bet is to use a company, that way no one gets hurt. Here, for example, this chemical corporation. We can easily siphon off four million. A million apiece. Agreed?" The others nodded mutely and reverently. "Now I'll transfer the four million to a numbered account in Switzerland. I did a job for them once, too, and I get in with the code word PRINCE CHARMING." "I had no idea you were such a romantic," Lothar said. "There're lots of things you don't know about me," Gabriele said frostily. "Okay. Now the money is in Switzerland, it's vanished. Now we only have to withdraw it again, but secretly, otherwise we've got the tax man breathing down our necks." She smiled at the others. "Each of us opens an account in four different Swiss banks, I transfer the money from the numbered account to these new ones and that's that. Is that all clear?" "Not in the least," Carmen said. "Lothar, you pack the computer and I'll pack my bag." Gabriele disappeared from the room. The three were completely taken aback. Werner whispered: "She wants some excitement in her life, just like I told you." And Lothar whispered back: "She was never this way before." Carmen said: "Werner, tell me the truth. What did you do with her?" "Nothing, my natural charm. That's all." He grinned. Carmen was disconcerted. Suddenly she threw her arms around Werner's neck and kissed him passionately. Werner was bewildered. "That's what you get," said Carmen.

. . .

To cross the border with Lothar, they had to hide him in the fridge in the RV, and when the guard decided to inspect the RV, Gabriele joined him and asked whether he wanted something to drink. She flung open the fridge, where Lothar sat chattering with cold, took out a soda and offered it to the guard. He was very taken by Gabriele, accepted the soda and dispensed with the search.

*Oh, I don't want to hear another word about beautiful or not beautiful. Gabriele thinks she's downright ugly, she says her neck is too long and her nose too big and that's why she has no luck with men. It didn't bother my Werner, but I'm not going to ask about it, I don't want to hear how passionately savage and wild he was with her, purring like an old tomcat. She envies us for our "fulfilled life," whatever the hell she means by that. She confided to me that Lothar has a complex because he hasn't got any hair on his arms like a real man. Werner has hair all over, a regular jungle of it. They would be a good match, but Lothar doesn't want anything to do with her. You've got to force happiness down his throat, I told her. She didn't know how, but I knew what to tell her, that Lothar only cares about money, and then she cried a little bit, tears in those big blue eyes, I really felt for her, although that's not at all what I intended. She loves him with or without hair, she said. She wants to use the money for a nose job. I can have the fat on my thighs sucked out, Gabriele*

*says. Sometimes it depresses me a little, because nothing really*
*helps in the end. I've always had an image of myself, like a*
*photograph, but just in my head, not a real one, how I would*
*have liked to be, someday, beautiful and slender of course,*
*but there was something else too that I can't explain so easily.*
*As if I had climbed to the top, and could see everything*
*below, and you do that with money, I thought. At some point*
*Werner and the kids were in the picture too, someday, when*
*all the bills have been paid, when there's nothing in our way,*
*when we're finally on top. But if someone would take a picture*
*of us, of two millionaires, me in my fur coat and Werner in*
*his gorgeous suit, you could tell from the photograph that we*
*were in disguise, that it was all wrong, we'd just look touch-*
*ing, that's it exactly, touching. And that's the same thing*
*as stupid, ridiculous, leaves them dying with laughter. How*
*I'd love to be someone else, can't anyone understand that?*

They opened their accounts in four different banks
and as the sun set they parked the RV on a mountain
with a view of the Alps. While Gabriele sat in the
camper at the computer and transferred millions, Lothar, Werner and Carmen discussed what they were
going to do with all their money. "I'm going to invest
it," Lothar said, "in real estate. Hot money's great
for that. And you two?" And as if with one voice,
Carmen and Werner said, "Pay off the house." "Oh
God," Lothar groaned, "how boring, can't you think
of anything else?" "I'd love to go back to work . . . "

Werner said softly. "More than anything in the world." "Then buy yourself the toy factory," Lothar said dryly. "They're in such rotten shape that all you have to do is slip half a mill under the table and they'll be ecstatic." A grin crept over Werner's face. "Do you think it'd work?" "Yes, of course. How often do you suppose they came to me at the bank and tried to dump the place? They're bankrupt, but it can be all yours." Werner simply glowed as no one had ever seen him glow before.

Gabriele came back from the camper. "Okay. Finished. We're rich." They all hugged. Then Gabriele said: "I have something to say. I didn't do it for the million. I don't care about the money. I have just one little condition. Otherwise I'll blow the whole deal. And the condition is you." She pointed at Lothar. "Me?" said Lothar aghast. "Yes. You've got to try it with me. For six months. I can't make you love me. But I can make you give it a try." Lothar looked at her in bewilderment. Then Werner said: "Well, Carmen forced my good luck down my throat, too." Lothar was silent, silent, silent, then he clutched his heart, walked over to Gabriele and gave her a kiss. Werner and Carmen gazed at them, deeply moved. Lothar whispered in Gabriele's ear: "What a rotten beast you are." She smiled.

· · ·

They paid a call on the four banks, one after the other, and each of them came back out with a large briefcase. They sat in the RV and marveled at all the money, drank a bottle of champagne together and turned maudlin. "I'm going to miss you," Lothar said. "Can't you come for a visit?" Carmen asked. "I hardly think so. People would wonder about your relationship with Germany's most famous hostage." "Oh, that's easy enough," Werner said, "we happen to be Germany's most famous bank robbers."

They drove to the nearest police station. "Just remember, you were wearing a blindfold the whole time," Gabriele said. "You don't know where you were the whole time. I'll keep an eagle eye on your money for you. That way you'll come back." Lothar climbed out. In the rearview mirror he grew smaller and smaller. He waved, then walked into the police station. "I've really gotten to like him, our local bank manager," Carmen said. Werner glanced at her suspiciously. She could feel the look and poked him in the ribs. "We played Scrabble." "Ha"—Gabriele laughed—"and Werner and I played video games." "I don't believe a word of it," Carmen said.

*She'd love to be like me, imagine that. "A natural beauty," she calls it, "coming from within." I'm so genuine, down-*

to-earth, no vanity, all modesty. Sounds like instant mashed potatoes. And she stared at me so earnestly the whole time, and for one brief moment I thought, could it be that the picture she has created of herself looks like me? I'd love to have a print of it, I'd frame it and hang it over my bed. I almost fell for it. But then she got up and looked in the mirror and said absolutely horrified: "Just look at that, I'm getting a deep wrinkle across my forehead," and I took a very careful look, I would have loved to see it, but there was nothing there. All the same, though, I like her, I really do, there's something of an angel about her, she sort of hovers above you. But she can't tell me that she just played video games with Werner.

The three of them stood in the Zürich airport, briefcases in hand. Gabriele was flying back to her hometown, and Werner and Carmen to theirs. "I'm so afraid of customs," Carmen said. "Aw, go on, we'll just walk right through cool as cucumbers. They're not going to search a good-looking, solid married couple like us." Carmen looked at Werner in amazement. They hugged Gabriele good-bye. On the way to the gate they passed a newspaper stand. Every magazine had a picture of Lothar on the cover, and the bold headlines celebrated their bank robberies. "Werner, would you ever have thought we'd be so famous someday?" Carmen remarked.

•   •   •

They walked hand in hand through the development, carrying their briefcases, heading home, and as Carmen was unlocking the door, Werner took her in his arms and carried her over the threshold. "Into our new life," he said. They shared a long kiss, and when they glanced up, there stood the kids. They looked completely different, were wearing torn, rumpled clothes, Rainer looked like a punk-rocker. They stared at their parents, Carmen in her expensive fur, Werner in his silk suit, and parents and children spoke as if with one voice: "What happened to you?"

A few months later, Carmen walked through the toy factory, along the conveyor belts where dolls now rolled by and fantastic dollhouses, gigantic stuffed animals and bright wading pools. People nodded respectfully to her. She went into the main office, sat down at her desk, sorted the mail, arranged a tray with coffee and added a newspaper. Her eyes fell on the front page. It read: GERMANY'S MOST FAMOUS HOSTAGE TO MARRY. Beneath it was a photo of Lothar Fuchs, and the caption beneath the photo read: "His traumatic experience as a hostage behind him, Lothar Fuchs, recently promoted to president of VG Bank, plans to wed Gabriele Gessmann, a housewife."

•   •   •

Carmen carried the tray and the newspaper into the boss's office. Werner looked imposing sitting there behind his desk. He was on the phone. Carmen kissed him and held the paper under his nose.

They were a little late getting there. Lothar and Gabriele were already at the altar. Without exception, the wedding guests looked classy, mainly bankers and their wives probably. Carmen whispered into Werner's ear: "They're suuuuch a beautiful couple." And when the rings were exchanged, she cried a little.

There was a surge of organ music, and the newly wed couple came slowly down the aisle toward them. They didn't spot Carmen and Werner until they were almost directly in front of them. They looked around in terror, as if they expected to be arrested right there in church. But when nothing happened, Lothar and Gabriele began to smile, and as they passed they gave Carmen and Werner inconspicuous, but firm, handshakes.

*From a distance they were both really gorgeous, a regular fairy-tale couple, both of them, very romantic. But then they got close to us, and Gabriele had great big circles under her eyes, and her hair wasn't shiny blond like normal, but sort of yellow and dull, Lothar has a spare tire, I spotted it right off, and his hairline's receding on both sides too. They didn't look all that happy, I was a little disappointed by that. Werner says I'm never satisfied, nonsense, I just wanted to admire them. Werner looked so snazzy in his tux, the other gentlemen all nodded to us, when we didn't know a soul, but they nodded to us as if we belonged. I should be satisfied, I know. But then, last night, I couldn't sleep, I don't know quite why either, we haven't a care in the world now, and I wandered through the house in my nightie and suddenly I felt so unhappy, for no reason.*

*Finally I went out to the garage, our new RV, the one Werner bought, is in there, and I got in and waited. But no one came. I hadn't the vaguest who was supposed to come really, so then I imagined I was an acrobat, and all the other performers had come by after my act to tell me how wonderful I had been up there on my tightrope, but that wasn't all that much fun either, so I gave a short try at being a hooker, they work out of RV's too you know, but all the men looked like Lothar, just tall and handsome, I sent them all packing, even though they pleaded with me, offered tons of money.*

*Then I cried a little, for no reason at all.*

*I'm back in the house, I snuggled up real close to Werner, he woke up, and we did it. It really was beautiful.*

# Paradise

We had got into the habit of taking little weekend excursions. Not saying a word, we would drive through the countryside, explore bleak, somber woods, trudge across dingy meadows, always with some goal, that next rise, that lake. We were fleeing. We never said so, but we both knew it.

We had met while we were students, everyone noticed her with her long, thick, shining blond hair—she was lovelier going away than coming toward you. Angelika.

Her mother's pride and joy, that hair, on the way to school some boys pulled her cap off, you always see women in commercials zooming onto the screen in their motorcycle helmets and racing caps, and then they take them off and a regular flood of golden hair gushes out, like salvation itself; the boys were pulling Angelika's hair, and that's where Lotte Kovacz came in, in Angelika's stories, a rough-and-tumble farm girl who wore crocheted sweaters and had a practical pigtail, who had never exchanged a single word with Angelika before, even though they were in the same class together, suddenly there stood Lotte Kovacz, facing a whole pack of boys, flashing a pocketknife and screaming: "You cowards! No pinching, no scratching, no hair pulling!" pushed up the sleeve of her pullover and cut deep into her own flesh. The boys backed off, impressed, and Angelika dressed Lotte's wound with maple leaves, because Lotte knew about that from stories about Indians. From then on she was Angelika's bodyguard.

Only much later, when I realized that my role in Angelika's life was solely that of guardian, did I re-member the story, and I asked myself what had made Lotte court Angelika and fight for her like that; how did Angelika manage to get people to leap into battle for her without giving a thought to their own injuries? I no longer wanted to.

She had never once expressed a wish to see Hissdorf again. Her family had left the place when she was twelve. Her father, a local teacher, had been trans-ferred to a small town, and there was only the barest trace of her having grown up in the country, she had a green thumb and didn't like house pets.

.    .    .

But today she suddenly demanded we drive to Hissdorf, it wasn't far at all, she said, and suddenly got
all excited, in a way I haven't seen her for a long time
now, and she acted as if it had long been her deepest
wish to see the village again. You may be disappointed,
it's probably completely changed, but she jumped
down my throat, no one could ever change her Hissdorf. Even after eleven years of marriage, I was hurt
by the crude, abrupt way she said it.

An ugly jerkwater place, set on a hill, bisected by a
federal highway, renovated farmsteads, their doorways
made of glass-block, the local tavern, The Stag, was
closed, the church, a clumsy affair with no charm
whatever.

Naturally she was disappointed, I could see that. She
sat there, silent and motionless, as I drove up and
down the main street a few times, until she pointed
to a modern single-family home: "There, that's where
our house was, and that's where Lotte lived." Directly
across the street, a ramshackle farmstead, the windowpanes blank, no compost heap at the door, apparently uninhabited, but all the same I urged Angelika to get out and knock, just maybe Lotte would
open the door. "Lotte? No, I don't even want to
know what's become of her, it would only make me

depressed." (I hate that word, Angelika uses it constantly, pops it into her mouth like a chocolate-covered cherry, her depression.)

She wanted to go home, and so I turned the car around, she wasn't even looking out the window now, was rummaging in her coat pockets for a cigarette, and without her asking, I stopped at a tiny grocery atop a low ridge just outside of Hissdorf.

She climbed out, without a word, I still liked her, from behind—that's awful, you could never tell anybody that. The tin-can decor behind the two small windowpanes was thick with dust, the labels faded. I liked her when her hair was wet. I liked her when she was asleep. Next to the house was a small pond, along its banks a couple of straggling daffodils bloomed. Somebody must have stuck some bulbs in the ground in the fall, why did so many people move to the country, to this leaden solitude and these musty villages? Angelika was taking her time getting cigarettes, I suddenly felt a craving for chocolate. It was seven steps from car to door, I still count them in my dreams.

They were embracing and didn't notice me. They murmured softly to each other, and Angelika kept stroking the other woman's hair, mousy-gray, shaggy,

I couldn't see her face at all, she was shorter than Angelika.

I don't know why I found the whole situation so embarrassing, almost as if I had caught Angelika in bed with another man; as I was considering how I could disappear without being seen, Angelika turned around and said, her face aglow: "This is Lotte." So that's her, a small, plain woman in a ghastly checked smock, very large brown eyes, irony about the mouth. (Is there such a thing as irony in the country? Beg your pardon, but that's what I was thinking at that moment.)

"And that's him?" A bare-boned, but perfectly normal, question, all the same Angelika broke into raucous laughter, Lotte let her laugh for a long time until she said, very slowly and with emphasis: "What are you laughing at? Isn't he worth much?" Angelika wasn't even trying to control herself, I figured it was time to introduce myself, I approached her with my hand outstretched, she backed off, that I still remember quite well, not fearfully, but she backed off, maybe without even taking a single step.

"I'm Jakob Göttlich," I said, and I'm used to everybody grinning at my "divine" last name, she just nodded earnestly, and searched my eyes as if I were introducing myself as her future son-in-law. This inane encounter disconcerted me completely, no, not with Lotte Kovacz, I mean Angelika, whom I didn't recognize at all, who had suddenly slipped away from me, her face red as a beet, and kept tossing her hair behind her, laughing and giggling. Lotte now crossed her arms across her chest: "He doesn't look too shabby." How could anybody talk like that? It was stuffy in the store, I was tugging at my scarf like a madman, what an idiotic statement, there was no way you could defend yourself, let alone offer a reply. She was staring at me, I would have loved to roll up like a bug and play dead. With a good, firm step, I should have headed out of the store, then and there.

In the meantime, Angelika had walked around behind the counter to where a thick book lay open, she sat down on the stool, I wanted to shout, wait, you can't sit there, that's Lotte's stool, she leafed through the book: "What's this, Lotte, you're reading Flaubert?" "Oh"—and all the while Lotte kept looking me in the eye—"is that how you pronounce it? I've always said Flaubert (and she in fact said it like 'flow,' rhymes with *cow*, and 'Bert'), never had any French. . . ." and at that Angelika was again convulsed with laughter. Was Lotte smiling at me?

She finally threw us out, she had some things to do; okay? We staggered toward the car like drunks, Angelika seemed at ease, melting with ease. We said nothing more about Lotte. She went to her publishing house, I to the zoological institute, meeting again that evening, silent, friendly, reserved. My cowardice was like an abscess somewhere deep within my body, and I tried to live with the illness, that's the advice you always read, just don't go crazy, don't let yourself start running amok. I knew it was a fatal illness, and all the while a totally normal life, a life with no catastrophes or blows of fate, no want, no reason whatever to complain.

Nothingness seems harder to bear than habits you hate; in bed we always lay in each other's arms, and as we lay there, I asked Angelika how a woman like Lotte, who had nothing really except that lousy grocery store, how she, a farm kid with a high-school education, would get the notion to read Flaubert, of all people. And in asking, I feared Angelika's anger, it was forbidden, it seemed, to talk about Lotte, but she replied very dryly, that it didn't surprise her at all, even as a child Lotte had had a nose for "that other world," of course she didn't understand what she was reading, and the way she had pronounced Flaubert! but for Lotte it was enough to know that it was rather exceptional for a country grocery clerk to be reading such books.

. . .

I didn't respond to that, held Angelika tighter in my arms, because I really didn't like her when she was like this, she had been talking about herself, not about Lotte, for although she surrounded herself with literature day in, day out, I always had the feeling that she never plumbed its secrets, had no real craving for it, she wolfed down books like a peasant in a three-star restaurant devouring a meal that doesn't taste all that good to him, he's sampling the stars, nothing more.

I pretended I would have to work very late at the institute, the way people always do. I read recently that an American entrepreneur had built a telephone with a button for blending in the appropriate "background noise excuse," the hubbub of voices at the airport, the mutterings of the meeting, here, honey, just listen for yourself, and you don't need to wait dinner for me.

I didn't consider myself especially original, I'm a bad liar, it's an effort.

She was sitting behind the counter, hardly looked up as I entered and the bell on the door jingled. I stood there sort of lost among the baker's chocolate and cans of fancy peas, she just had to finish this page, a tractor drove by.

. . .

"Last time you looked like you wanted to beat a hasty retreat. Why did you come back?" She twirled a strand of hair in her fingers, didn't stand up, and so I sat on the counter, noticed how dirty her smock was, and how white her arms. I told her the truth, how astonished I'd been by Angelika's transformation, she hadn't laughed like that for ages, but that I hadn't liked the laughter much, especially the stupid part about pronouncing French. Oh, that hadn't bothered her at all, just the opposite, back in school, Angelika had always liked to correct her.

"So you thought you'd give her a treat?" "Oh, the poor thing didn't know what she should say, really . . . I've got a dictionary . . ." I could scarcely believe how easily she had wrapped Angelika around her finger, her self-assurance suddenly repelled me, I was about to defend Angelika, but now she was saying how Angelika had been her only friend in life. "You trying to tell me you haven't a friend in the world?" I broke in with a smile. "Why did you come?" she abruptly asked again, and then she fell silent and stared at me.

I could claim Lotte Kovacz raped me. It was she, after all, who slammed her book shut and locked up. Her room above the store was small and crammed with bookcases sagging beneath the classics of world literature. Through the window I could see the little pond and the daffodils.

Her skin was white and soft, except that her hands were cracked and leathery, they wandered over me all on their own, detached from Lotte, who said not a word, didn't even smile, but gave herself to her task like no other women I've ever encountered.

I saw the scar on her forearm, but all the same for me Lotte was like a fantasy of my own invention.

I heard myself speaking soft, impossible sentences about eternal love and passion, I didn't know that you can invent emotions, but that is how it was, that evening I invented my grand passion.

She didn't respond, she didn't have to, either. I loved her flesh, thick, white, soft flesh, so very strange, the moves I had practiced with Angelika all those years didn't seem to fit here, they were too small, too shy.

She didn't say another word until long after it was over. "Explain to me how it's possible for a man to describe the innermost heart of a woman. . . ." Would you believe she started talking about *Madame Bovary*? She repeated her question, as if it were her chief concern in life, and I babbled something stupid about fantasy and the female side of a man and vice versa, about yin and yang, which I shouldn't have done, because she wanted to know precisely where you could read about that. With a ballpoint that lay on her nightstand, I drew the yin-yang symbol for her on her belly. She smiled, and a wave of tenderness surged over me like a Pavlovian reflex.

So that was that, a fossilized scientist, married, in love with a country lass, her cheeks red as roses, her skin white as snow ... Wind and rain had already put some creases in her face, yet she looked younger than Angelika. She got up, dressed in silence, I lay there, naked and helpless, feeling like a cliché.

Did she have a bathroom, I wondered? I would have liked to wash up, but didn't want to ask for fear of offending her. "There's a sink behind the store, just cold water," she said, as if guessing my thoughts, and "Why are you so embarrassed?" All the while looking at me so calm and cool, and I would gladly have told her how I wasn't embarrassed in the least, and that it was she after all who had locked up the store and taken me by the hand and led me upstairs, but she was on her way out of the room now, very graceful, mocking.

·   ·   ·

When I came downstairs, she was sitting behind the counter again and reading, as if nothing had happened, there was nothing more to say, I hung around, came close to thanking her even.

"You'll try to come back again. I'd rather you didn't."

"No, no, I won't come back," I stammered like a dunce.

"But you'll try."

"Why should I?"

"Because you think you've discovered something."

"Aha. And what's that?"

"I really don't know."

"I won't come back."

"Then everything's fine."

And all of it without ever once looking up from her damned Flaubert. I had been dismissed, and so finally I left, and the store bell jangled behind me.

The drive home. Rain. Rotten visibility. Is there even a chance of not making an idiot of yourself, isn't it rather that we make idiots of ourselves every day, marching off punctually to work, living with women we don't love, fathering children that, before they're born, we think will be our joy in life? (I've always held it against Angelika that she didn't want any.) I was already looking for excuses.

. . .

I really didn't enter the grocery store again, that I didn't do. Through its dirty windows, I watched her sitting there, sometimes long after closing time, and once she had turned out the light downstairs, I could see her moving back and forth in her room. I hid by the pond, behind some thorny underbrush that kept ripping my jacket, always had a second pair of shoes along. I don't think I ever thought myself so ridiculous, crouching there with my feet sinking ever deeper into the mud, shivering with cold. It was enough for me to see her, and the more I hung around her store, the more incomprehensible her life seemed to me.

That first week I waited for her lover. She had to have one, some married farmer maybe, who arrived on his bike and parked it behind the house so as not to give himself away. But she had no visitors, except for a salesman now and then, or kids who dawdled home with big bags of candy, as if the way to the store and back were a stay of execution.

Twice a week, just before six, a delivery van arrived, and in my mind's eye I could already see a strapping young fellow get out and the two of them disappear into her room, that would have solved everything, but the driver was a fat guy around fifty, who leaned on his van and smoked and watched her drag the crates and boxes into the store. She gave him a beer.

. . .

Maybe some girlfriends visited her of a morning, and so for over a week I took mornings off, left the car on a dusty lane some distance off, slunk across meadows and fields, kept a safe distance, wishing fervently I had some binox, but I didn't want to do that to her.

No girlfriends. Sometimes some guy driving by would stop, and each time I waited for him not to come out of the store, jealousy pounced on me like a mangy dog, but there he would be again, setting his motor howling, the way people do in the country.

I was nicer to Angelika than perhaps ever before, well okay, at the very beginning I had been enchanting, I rediscovered some positive things about her, once even felt the spontaneous urge to go to bed with her, didn't act on it though, that seemed downright perverse, was I going to cheat on Lotte?

Summer came around. I had to fight off the mosquitos lurking around the pond like a bomber squadron.

I could only drive out there late in the evening now, cursing daylight-saving time. Lotte liked to sit and read on the bench behind the house these days, for as long as the light lasted.

. . .

I did risk it once, belly-crawling my way through the grass, the way I had learned in the army in bygone days, she glanced my way a few times, and I went dizzy at the thought she might spot me and despise me forever.

During that period, nothing excited me more than to watch Lotte alone with herself, and her self-enforced isolation turned me and everyone I knew in the city into wild-eyed cardboard cutouts.

One day, in the middle of the week, a sign, scrawled in a childish hand, was hanging on the shop door: Closed, something I didn't discover until it was dark, not a light was burning anywhere in the house and I risked a hesitant approach. Great anxiety engulfed me at once. I waited for her until midnight, finally drove sadly home, feeling as if I had just lived one whole day in vain.

At home, there was a vase on the table, a single daffodil in it. Without greeting Angelika, I walked over and gingerly touched it. Plastic. A plastic flower. Angelika had strange tastes. She seemed relaxed, in good spirits, didn't ask, as she usually did, what I'd been doing till that hour, no, she had even kept dinner warm, and while I ate it in silence, she smiled inscrutably to herself, said she had a surprise for me after dinner.

She took me by the hand, crept on tiptoe to the bedroom door, laid a finger to her lips, two little kids on Christmas morning. Lotte lay in my bed. She was sound asleep, one fist clenched up to her face. Could I sleep on the couch perhaps, Angelika whispered. She was acting as if someone had given her a present.

Yes, Lotte had closed her shop or rented it, wanted to move into town, heaven knew why, but that's what she had got into her head. "And when Lotte wants something . . ."

"Where's she going to live?" I knew the answer before I got it.

"Oh, I thought, with us at first, if you don't mind. It'd be nice to have a little company, you're never around, and besides, she needs someone to look after her. She hasn't the least notion how she's going to manage here."

Angelika went on talking, but her words were no longer reaching my ears, once again I thought of fleeing, of tugging my suitcase out of the closet and getting out of this apartment, not because of Lotte, whose presence made it seem as if I hadn't been keeping tabs on my own fantasies, they had got totally out of control and had materialized on me, no, what I couldn't bear was the thought of Angelika, compared to Lotte she seemed to me like some terrifying alien for whom I felt only shame.

I hardly slept that night, thought of the two of them there in the bedroom, and was certain that at that very moment Angelika was lifting the cover, bending down over Lotte and looking for the scar on her arm. I opened the door, and there they lay, sound asleep, and Angelika had thrown her arm across Lotte's breast, as if unintentionally, as if in a dream. I couldn't bring myself to breakfast with them, crept out of the apartment very early in the morning, heading for the lab, thinking I could find a solution under the microscope, a solution to what? I had been robbed of my daily visit to Lotte, and already I missed it the way an alcoholic misses his bottle.

I drank some courage, holding out till five o'clock, and ran home as if bloodhounds were on my trail.

She was alone, sitting on the sofa. I didn't ask about Angelika, the world's most unimportant question, I stood at the door, silent and stiff, and she said very softly, so softly I almost didn't understand her, that now I wouldn't have to drive that long distance, not to mention the mosquitos around the pond . . .

. . .

I gently laid a hand on her shoulder, she sat there calm as could be and let me. Angelika came home from shopping.

I couldn't get used to the three of us living together. The sleepless nights on the sofa drifted past, and come morning my palms were drenched with sweat, my thoughts tangled.

At the breakfast table, Lotte would eye me without a word; Angelika would babble away, talking about Lotte as if she were a doll someone had given her, a doll that could do everything, almost human. She had impulsively put Lotte on a diet, she really was in impossibly bad shape, and to make things easier for her, we all got diet-crisps for breakfast. We nibbled away noisily, and an amused Lotte, or so it seemed to me, put up with Angelika.

Sometimes, abruptly and totally out of context, she would open her mouth and lob questions at me, always just me, like Molotov cocktails, her aim was perfect, and, totally unprepared, I feared them. "Are you happy living like this?" Imagine that at breakfast, or "How can anyone live together so intimately with someone for years on end?" Yes, she was genuinely interested to learn "how you do that" and then the constant ghastly questions about love, what did I understand by it, whether I had such a feeling for Angelika every day or just once a year maybe, she harped on it like a child, wouldn't let up on it, and while I agonized over my answers, making references to love in novels, Angelika would lean back as if she were watching television, and break into a peal of laughter every time. I couldn't put Lotte off with literary allusions, she understood them well enough, but such descriptions of passion were just figments of imagination, she wanted to know whether all that existed in reality, because nobody lives the way people do in novels.

It was gruesome, I fled to the institute, helpless, wounded to the quick, a raw hunk of meat, it wouldn't have taken much and I'd have burst into tears. How did she manage it, a stupid hick with the emotions of a five-year-old? And yet there was nothing I longed for more than to be alone with Lotte, and so I pleaded with Angelika to finally find Lotte a room somewhere, I could put up with her no longer, and wanted above all to be alone again with her, Angelika. I had long ago turned into a liar.

Angelika just smiled, what I couldn't put up with, she suggested, were Lotte's questions, I finally had no answers, and that was good for me, I'd see soon enough.

I didn't have the sense that Lotte liked Angelika all that much; as far as I could tell, she regarded her with the same mockery she did me. What did she want with us, anyway?

Around noon one day, bending over my microscope, I began to get a rotten headache, decided to go home, and at every step the wish grew stronger that Angelika would not be there.

With every step up the stairs, I counted it out, "Lotte is alone," "Lotte is not alone," like a schoolboy, when my greatest joy had been to be alone in the house.

Both of them were gone. I accepted the disappointment, deciding that at least I could lie down in my, in her bed and find the scent of her on the pillow, and there she lay totally nude, as if expecting me, how idiotic, how could she know . . . ? She smiled, and I was out of my clothes before I knew what I was doing. She smelled of Angelika's perfume, and I held that against Angelika. She flung her arms around my neck and I stammered a couple of phrases I knew only from books, words that had never passed my lips before. I didn't see Angelika until she was standing beside the bed, and no fear coursed through my body, just an immense cold spread over me, rendering me completely insensitive, indifferent, and so I just calmly got up, not embarrassed at all, asked Angelika to let me by, opened up the closet, naked as a jaybird, and threw my shirts and suits onto the bed, at Lotte's feet, who was watching me with a face devoid of expression. Only now, as I pulled the suitcase out of the closet, did Angelika find words, screamed, her voice snapping with agitation, for me to pack my bags right now, she was throwing me out of the house, all of which was quite unnecessary, I was already on my way.

Lotte stood up, stretched, I swear, she stretched and said to Angelika: "You're late. We were going to go into town, you know." She didn't give me so much as a glance. I've thought a great deal about that sentence since.

Suddenly every bit of nervousness was gone. I had taken the first step. I moved into a small studio, even enjoyed my solitude, having convinced myself that Lotte had forced this turn of events so that afterward she could have me all to herself. Lotte. She didn't come.

A week later, I drove along my old street, as if by accident, and then I found myself in the parking lot catercorner to our apartment, evening after evening, and as I sat there time and space blurred. I can no longer say how long I stuck it out, until at last I saw them leaving the house together one evening, a total shock, because at first I took Lotte for a stranger, her hair was dyed platinum blond, she was wearing some sinfully expensive getup of Angelika's, which I vaguely recognized, and spike heels that were obviously giving her trouble.

Angelika wanted to take her revenge out on me, that's the only way I could figure this change in Lotte at that moment, I imagined hurling myself at Angelika, hitting her, choking her, I crept along behind the two of them, totally numb, and suddenly it was clear to me that I'd been given a sign: I had to rescue Lotte. Yes, I would personally give her back her hair color, her clothes, her figure and personality, that was my task, the first real task I'd ever had in life, so it seemed to me.

They made the rounds of tawdry bars in the neighborhood of the train station, that was sure to be Angelika's idea, she was too much a coward to do that on her own, although she always had had the notion that real life was someplace where she didn't know her way around.

I watched them make conversation with men whose

shirts were open to their navels, Lotte tugged playfully on the ear of one and teased another, she laughed with her mouth open wide and let a third one pinch her butt.

Only now did it strike me that next to Lotte, Angelika seemed rather withdrawn, she hadn't taken any particular pains with her makeup or hairdo, either; she looked like Lotte's little, uglier sister, who was leaving the field all to her, something totally unlike her. For Angelika, until now, in her effort to be the center of attention, every woman, no matter what she looked like, was a challenge, to battle if need be. There she sat perfectly calm, watching Lotte with a look of bliss on her face that was new to me. And as much as I hated her for what she had done to Lotte—and so to me—with this absurd costume, at that moment I liked her better than I ever had over the last few years.

I practically glued my nose to the windowpane and didn't split until a drunk threatened to punch me out, muttering something about how it wasn't proper to stare at other people like that, which was probably true, but I had long since lost any sense of what was proper or what wasn't, to be precise, since the day I saw Lotte for the first time. Me, who had always kept the world at a kind of ironic arm's length, of which I'd once been very proud, because it had kept me from sentimental foolishness, from being ridiculous.

She came in the middle of the night, knocked on my door. Emerging from deep sleep I opened up, for, as always, I had been waiting for her in my dreams.

She moved with more grace than she used to, smoked, too.

"You're carrying on worse than a stray dog." Those were her first words.

"Lotte, don't you really know why?"

She sat down on my bed and crossed her legs, and only now did it hit me that there were certain similarities between my studio and her room above the grocery. The bed stood facing the window, like hers, the way my room looked bare and messy at the same time, suddenly I knew that I had seen it all once before.

"Lotte, forgive the clichés, but I want nothing more than to have you with me. . . ."

"But don't you realize that I can't live with another person?" She sounded totally amazed, as if she were trying to explain fire to a child to keep it out of harm's way. Our conversation wandered as if in a dream, and I wasn't quite certain myself that all this was in fact happening, I had fantasized too long and too violently about it.

"Jakob! I live only in your imagination, you've fantasized a novel that I haven't read. . . ."

"Oh, you'd like to believe that, that way you make me invisible, that way you can murder me!"

"Tut, tut, tut . . . You talk about murder! What about Angelika? Have you ever thought what you've done to her . . . ?"

I interrupted her: "No, God knows I haven't. But it's high time that we . . ."

"Yes, you're right. Every minute we waste is one minute too many."

It was enough to drive me crazy, I didn't understand her, as if she were speaking a foreign language, but it was only when she spoke that I recognized my Lotte again, and so I trembled in fear of the moment when she might simply fall silent, the way she so often did. I sat at her feet, wanting to gently stroke her leg.

"And now you'll grab hold of me, so that you can feel something and then dream about it for weeks again." She tossed her platinum hair back, not all that adept at it yet, but so deliberate. How had she learned in such a short time to imitate Angelika so perfectly?

"Why did you have your hair dyed? Don't you realize that you look like Angelika now, like some bad copy of her?" She laughed at that and let herself fall back on the pillows, Angelika had predicted that I would say that.

"Angelika knows you're here?"

"Naturally. Why not?"

She sat back up and looked me in the eye.

"Tell me, Jakob, you've probably never done anything for someone else, have you? I can tell by looking at you, no, you've never sacrificed anything, given something up for someone else's sake . . ."

Hah, I had to laugh in her face, her transformation as a sacrifice she'd made for Angelika? "And what if I haven't? Why should I?" She repeated her question, which she must have picked up from one of her damn books, and now I grabbed tight hold of her arm.

"And why do you want to know? What would that change? And how do you measure a sacrifice? By how much pain it causes someone? If that's the case, then take a look at me. . . . I've given up my normal life for . . ."

She broke in: "For me?" She stood up and walked to the door, I wanted to throw myself between it and her and plead with her to stay with me at least for tonight, but I knew I couldn't stop her with that, I would have to give a real answer to her question, and the magic word wouldn't come to me. She didn't even turn around to look at me. She walked her scornful walk down the red-carpeted hall, withdrew from me like some idea that had not been thought through.

I spent the next few weeks as if in a fever. I had frittered away my chance, had lost before I'd even understood the rules of the game. Incapable of going to work, I lay in bed. What had made Lotte close her store and come to the city? What did she want? I racked my brains for her reasons, waxed philosophic: What sets a human being in motion other than life's basic needs? I shook that question hard, and only one thing fell out of it in answer: emotions. They had, after all, moved me to forget all scruples and morals, to leave a secure world of clear rules; they had turned me into an enthusiastic victim.

But did that go for Lotte as well? And if so, what emotions were those that caused her to get up from behind the counter and abandon her island, where I would so gladly have walked?

Every evening I stood in front of the building, but only twice was I able to spot them heading out on their excursions to red-lit bars, and then I saw only Angelika coming home from work, from shopping, from the cleaners. Had she forbidden Lotte to leave the house? I slipped like a thief into the stairwell, listened at the door to the apartment, my name had already been pasted over, but there wasn't the least sound to be heard.

After days of growing desperation, I threw myself across Angelika's path, up close she looked older than I remembered her, and much more earnest. She showed not the least surprise at seeing me, let me stammer my question about Lotte, and then said quite calmly: "She's gone."

I would have loved to shake her, but this woman could no longer be shaken, in my absence she had grown a second skin that made her impervious to the world, quite different from before. Where was Lotte? She gazed at me in pity, set down her plastic bags and pulled two photographs from her coat pocket. The one showed Lotte with her tangled mousy-gray hair, her old-fashioned clothes, the other a woman wearing heavy makeup sitting on a bar stool, spangles in her blond hair, her dress slit up to the thigh, a glass in her hand.

"There. That's what I've made of her. And now she's getting to know the world." She smiled. I cried out as if it were a matter of life and death: "You talked her into this!"

"Oh, my poor silly boy"—she walked toward her building—"do you really believe you can talk someone into something they don't totally and completely want themselves?"

I squeezed out of her that Lotte had wanted to move to a really big city. To some other country?

"No . . . Frankfurt, Hamburg, Berlin . . . what do I know?" I grabbed the pictures out of her hand, she let me have them the way you throw a dog a bone you've gnawed on long enough. She walked to the door, erect and self-assured, she was wearing flats, something she'd never done during the years with me.

I didn't even bother to quit my job. I withdrew half my savings, leaving the other half for Angelika, we had a joint account. I took a strange delight, even amid my abysmal despair over Lotte's disappearance, in being "fair." I've always been a good citizen, anxious never to take more than my due.

I hate traveling. The landscape flew by to no purpose. I had picked Berlin as my first city, because for me, more than any other German city, it smelled of the "big wide world," if that really was what Lotte had in mind.

At first I stayed at the Kempinski, but it soon became clear to me that it could take a while for me to find her, and so I moved into a small pension, rose every morning at eight and wandered the city.

I looked in every bar, stuck the two photographs under the nose of every waiter, no matter how unfriendly, and in return got silent shakes of the head, suspicious questions about whether I was a cop, sometimes curses, few of them took time to give the pictures a closer look.

I was no longer aware of the days, or of the nights. I would comb the city until exhaustion drove me back to my hotel. At one point my landlady whispered to me over breakfast that I really ought to shave and get a haircut, a handsome young man like me. I moved out.

It turned cold, I wanted to buy a pair of warmer shoes. The salesgirl ripped the pair I had selected out of my hands, they were definitely too expensive for me. I finally took the ones she brought me and slipped on with disgust, ugly brown things that made my feet look awful, but I was in no condition to argue with this salesgirl; everyone around me seemed in some miraculous way to be powerful and confident of victory.

Sometimes it was an effort to speak a simple sentence, I began to stutter, and then I would feel profound sympathy for this Jakob Göttlich, who was at the mercy of universal ridicule, who grew weaker and weaker, a social outcast. Jakob, I said to the poor wretch, don't worry about it, you're living for a goal, you're fighting, and if you perish in the attempt, your goal is worth it.

It didn't bother me, in fact, that I was going to the dogs, on the contrary. When two youths mugged me in Kreuzberg one evening, relieving me of every penny I had on me, I merely felt myself strengthened in my purpose, wasn't angry or desperate, but instead, I interpreted this event as a test, a sign that I should persevere, come what may.

In a sleazy dive where now and again I would stop for a beer on my rounds, two men were sitting behind me trading stories about their whorings. I tried not to listen, felt embarrassed for my own sex at the way they were bragging to each other.

It didn't dawn on me until long after they had left. "Then she showed me a picture," one of them had said, "a snapshot of the way she used to look, you wouldn't believe! A regular chick from the sticks, from Bavaria no less. Fifty a throw. But let me tell you it was worth it." I bolted for the street, hoping to thank them, shake their hands with tears in my eyes, pay them a finder's fee. They had vanished.

.   .   .

She was climbing into a truck with a Wuppertal license. All I saw were her legs, but I was certain I had found her.

For days I lived off that triumph, felt no need at all to rush off to talk with her; I rode past her in a taxi. Her hair still platinum-blond, she stood there on the street like a torch, very erect, very nonchalant, buoyant.

In front of a department store, I struck up a conversation with a young, quite respectable-looking fellow who was sitting there with hat in hand and a sign at his belly, he had been released from prison and was hungry. A damn charming liar, I found him not un-attractive, which was important. He listened to my proposal with a smirk and accepted, glaring at me as if I were the dregs of humanity. I counted out my last two hundred marks for him, giving not the least thought to how I was going to live in the days ahead.

He was playing it close to the chest, I had to worm everything out of him, she was very aloof despite her profession, strange somehow, "like an elegant lady," that put him off a little, but she was "good," he "couldn't complain," and he'd be glad to pay her even more frequent visits, and held his hand out as he said it. I asked him if I could finish the rest of his french fries, he shoved them at me contemptuously.

. . .

Maybe I was hoping he'd say that she whispered my name as she lay in his arms, absurd, I know, but I wasn't going to relinquish my last glimmer of hope that there was at least some memory of me in her body. (Was there something of Angelika in my own? It was an effort now for me to recall her face, almost as if there had never been an Angelika, or as if I had only stuck it out with her so long in order to meet Lotte Kovacz.)

She came to see me, and it was pointless to ask how she knew that I was in town or how she'd got the name of my hotel. She simply came and brought me a hot meal in paper containers, early one morning. I ate greedily and gazed steadily at her. She scolded me softly, tenderly almost, for letting myself get into such a sorry state. Because I had been forced to watch her degrade herself, and would she please explain to me how she could even . . . She just shook her head at that. "But you're the one who brought me to this, you know," and once again I didn't understand at all, yes, she insisted, I had dragged her out of her grocery, into the city, to people like this, and in her mouth that sounded like "to this zoo." I had in fact never once let her out of my sight, until she realized that that was my way of daring her to live among other people, to let people observe her, and that's precisely what she was doing now, and she was happy discovering for herself all the things that she had only read about before. Aha, now she was playing Camille, I thought, she wouldn't listen to logic, snatched at each one of my sentences as if it were a bothersome fly in the air, batted it down.

"Jakob, why can't you understand that I have to move on whenever you show up?" How was I supposed to understand that, when I only came to bring her back with me, to be with her, finally, really.

Laughter. Then did she have no feelings for me at all? I asked like a schoolboy with his first crush, and she thought it over for a long time, my heart started to flutter now.

"No, I don't think so, but I don't know if a person can have any feelings at all for someone else, you have those for yourself and for nobody else." Ah, what could I reply to that, Lotte had discovered the phenomena of projection and transference, banalities, and yet, the way she presented her discoveries, each one came wrapped in the charm of her earnestness.

"But, Lotte, I love you. It's that simple."
    "Yes, I know," she said curtly and gathered up the paper containers. "I'm getting out of Berlin."

"I'll follow you."

She sat down next to me, caressing my arm, she'd learned that in those trucks, a gesture that didn't suit her at all. "That won't make you happy."

"And you? Men, who don't want anything from you except your body? They despise you, and it'll break you."

"Oh, no, they want something else entirely, they just can't express it. . . ."

That got me mad, I stood up, ran wildly around the room, shouting so loud my neighbor banged on the wall, "So, you really think there are some little Flauberts among your johns, run-of-the-mill nobodies, that's what they are, who come to you for a quickie before going home to the wife and kids! What the hell do you think they want from you?"

"That's no way to talk about people, Jakob."

"Come on, tell me! What are they looking for, in your opinion?"

"An idea, some idea about the world, what really makes it go round . . ."

"Oho! What holds the world together at its core? You poor fool! That's literature! It's not Goethe who pays you your lousy fifty marks. Don't you get it? They take you the same way they bolt down food and booze. That's all!"

I raged, she watched me, smoothing the sheet with her hand. "Have you ever done it, Jakob?"

. . .

She paid my hotel bill, I was four weeks behind, left the landlady an extra five hundred marks, and then she was gone.

I learned from her co-workers that she had left for Hanover, they eyed me suspiciously, never making me an offer to try it with them, a little later I saw myself in a department-store mirror, and I understood. A lunatic was looking at me and nodding, there was no way back.

In Hanover she didn't work the streets, she had a room in a cathouse, an "Eros Center."

When I arrived, she had already arranged for a little studio for me, and she came every day to check on me, a new twist, and greater agony than anything I'd been through before. She brought me books that I never cracked, the sheer mockery of it, offering me literature the way you give kids jelly beans to hush their crying.

She decked me out in new clothes, cut my hair, shaved me, that was great fun, we went out to eat together, she paid, and was forever suggesting that I really ought to try writing, I was so clever, or, if that didn't suit me, go back to my old job. She didn't have a glimmer, didn't want to.

I am waiting for her. She arrives in a dazzling blue summer dress, pink sweet-peas in her arms, which she lays on my nightstand, she gives me a hug, a kiss on the cheek. We go for a walk, lie in a meadow lush with spring, I can smell her she is lying so close to me, and all of a sudden, anger seizes me, here, in the middle of the park, I'd like to strangle her, people out walking their dachshunds can stand and watch if they like, it would make no difference to me.

Day after day, I begged her to spend at least one night with me, what she did with other men, she could do with me, too, I was even ready to get a job so I could pay her. She just laughed at that, "Oh but, Jakob, they don't claim to be in love with me, don't you see that's why it won't work?"

At least she was using the informal pronoun with me now, and people might have thought we were the world's happiest couple as we walked along arm in arm window-shopping, asked me if she should buy a new dress, just for me, because her work clothes were quite different. When she came to see me, she put on prim, white cotton underwear, something she did just for me, really, stopped at least to think, what should I wear, I'm off to visit Jakob.

. . .

I ought to have known it wouldn't work, I had rented the wig from a costume shop, ditto the beard, didn't take off my sunglasses, and it did get me into her room, but she recognized me at once, which I would have had trouble doing myself, got very angry, the first time I'd ever seen her like that, trembling with rage, she was never going to visit me again, didn't want to see me again. Afterward every tree looked like a suicide tree.

It was a long time before I saw her again, a very long time. She bawled me out, I had no right to starve myself to death, no right whatever not to go on living, and what was I doing, grandstanding like this, all in all she had had it up to here with my self-pity, and she could lead a very "carefree" life without me around, what did I think I was doing. She didn't even know what that meant, a "carefree" life, living together with the person you love, going through life together with him. As I said it I vaguely recalled how at one time I would probably have burst into scornful laughter at such phrases, but that lay far in the past. She didn't laugh. "You can't go through life together, you go it alone, period. I don't ever want to hear it again, that's even more stupid than anything the girls spout." She was right, I was just bullshitting. She suggested what we needed was a really "carefree," there was that word again, toast to our farewell, with champagne. I believe it was at that moment that I thought, clearly and coolly, what a shame, she's turned normal.

But then I got drunk, and on the way home grabbed her roughly by the arm and wouldn't let go, and she didn't resist, even came upstairs with me, that should have made me suspicious; a single sentence kept whirling like mad through my brain: Now, now, you've made it. I don't recall the rest, only that I dreamed about her, dreamed about her lying naked next to me and running her fingers along my back, slowly, constantly, like letters of the alphabet on my back, except I couldn't decipher them, couldn't understand.

I woke up naked and alone. My arms and legs felt atrophied, my skull was rumbling as if someone had hit me over the head. I dragged myself to the sink, held my head under the tap, and then I turned around, full of dread, I still remember that. Very slowly I turned around, my back to the mirror, my whole body shaking, moved my head to look back over my shoulder. I'VE SET YOU FREE. GO. Dazzling red like her nail polish, backwards on the mirror. I must have fainted then. She was gone, no one knew where. I conducted the investigation like a police detective, distanced and with no personal involvement, of course she was gone, there had never been any doubt of that.

.   .   .

Hope had deserted me overnight. The veil was lifted.

They took me back at the institute without hesitation, asked polite questions about the illness from which I had presumably recovered now, thank God, and I provided friendly replies, yes, an illness that had been around for a long time but about which science still knew almost nothing, and we moved to the next item on the agenda.

I lived in a hotel, not wanting to settle in anywhere, or ever to have to say, this is *my* room, I live here, this is me. Each month I'd have them give me a new room, and when the first one came around again, I'd already forgotten it.

I forgot everything. Days, nights, seasons, forgot what I looked like, refused to let my eyes fix a hold on anything or anyone, made memories impossible.

I lived my life away.

Life spares a man nothing.

He sat down at my breakfast table, despite the little brass plate inscribed with his room number on a very nice table by the window. I was reading the paper, he disturbed me all the same. A man about my age, good-looking, he asked what sort of work I did, about my life-style, I was chary with my answers, but he soon considered himself my good friend.

It was on his account that I ate my breakfast in my room from then on, which I didn't want to do, I needed that breakfast room as a way to approach the world, to get myself in shape morning after morning, to become visible.

He startled me awake in the middle of the night, had brought a bottle of red wine along and was in the room before I could stop him. He had to tell me a story, he was somewhat embarrassed, I could see that clearly, he even blushed. I yielded, hoping it would soon be over with. I didn't touch the wine. It began with a perfectly harmless description of his marriage, boring like most, of his wife, none of which interested me in the least.

He was a salesman, pharmaceuticals, a college dropout, you see, that was important for his story, and so he traveled in rural areas a great deal, you could talk country doctors into a lot, and at that point I decided he should leave, right then, and I didn't ask him politely, but jumped up, flung open the door, he came up behind me, got a rough hold on me, shoved me against the wall, damn it all, I was going to hear the rest of this. A madman, I no longer tried to resist, knowing full well I'd have to pay for this.

A small store, he had wanted to get something to drink, it had been scorching hot, just a little, shoddy grocery store, I had to picture it. I didn't want to picture it. She had had long blond hair, incredible hair, had been sitting behind the counter, hadn't so much as smiled at him, otherwise he might have understood, a flirtation on a hot summer day. "She was reading," I said not intending to say anything, no, where did I get that, well maybe, he hadn't noticed it, but now that I mentioned it, yes, she had been reading. And now there was no turning back, no going home, even though his wife was nice enough, but that woman in the store, it was torture to him, and he had to keep going back there, she was arrogant and scary somehow, she was beyond your reach, and that was the worst part of it. The whole time he wore a lunatic smile.

I no longer know how I got there, by bus or maybe I hitchhiked. Pale yellow light from the store was shining on the road.

The moon stood above the house. Her hair was hanging down over her face, so she was still dyeing it, her arms propped up, one hand playing with a strand of hair.

. . .

As I stood there, a crystalline clarity pierced me. I had never felt that way before.

The door was open, to let in a breath of cool air I guess. I pulled off my shoes. My pulse slowed, suddenly I felt very calm. Slowly I groped along behind the display case. Oxtail soup, fancy green peas, beef goulash, I deliberately read each label, step by step, I drew nearer to her.

Maybe I stood behind her for a long time, maybe only briefly, twice she turned a page, I heard her breathing.

I strangled her with her own hair, long enough to go around her neck once and then some, thick, yellow hair, she didn't utter a sound, I hadn't expected it to be any other way.

Tenderly I caught her as she fell to one side, and then—no, I wasn't afraid, just amazed, and thought, so this, this is how the whole thing is resolved, so this is how it was supposed to end.

She looked different from what I remembered, but in fact I really had no memories of her at all now; no one will understand that, you were married all that time, Herr Göttlich, they'll say, and you claim you could no longer remember her?

I laid Angelika on the stone floor and covered her with my jacket.

I'll read Flaubert until they arrive.

A NOTE ABOUT THE AUTHOR

Doris Dörrie was born in Hanover, West Germany, in 1955. In addition to attending film school in Munich, she pursued her studies in the United States at the University of the Pacific in Stockton, California, and at the New School for Social Research in New York. Currently a resident of Munich, Ms. Dörrie's films include *Men*, *Paradise*, *Me and Him*, and *Money*. She has received awards in Moscow, Rio de Janeiro, Berlin and Tokyo.

A NOTE ON THE TYPE

The text of this book was set on the Monotype in a type face named Perpetua, designed by the British artist Eric Gill (1882–1940) and cut by The Monotype Corporation, London, in 1928–1930. Perpetua is a contemporary letter of original design, without any direct historical antecedents. The shapes of the roman letters basically derive from stonecutting, a form of lettering in which Gill was eminent. The italic is essentially an inclined roman. The general effect of the type face in reading sizes is one of lightness and grace. The larger display sizes of the type are extremely elegant and form what is probably the most distinguished series of inscriptional letters cut in the present century.

Composed by Crane Typesetting Service, Inc., Barnstable, Massachusetts. Printed and bound by The Haddon Craftsmen, Inc., Scranton, Pennsylvania.

Designed by Mia Vander Els

P9-EED-973

# ínspirations

# MODELLING CLAY

### Decorative projects to create for the home

**inspirations**

# MODELLING CLAY

Decorative projects to create for the home

# PENNY BOYLAN

## PHOTOGRAPHY BY TIM IMRIE

LORENZ BOOKS

First published in 1999 by Lorenz Books

Lorenz Books is an imprint of
Anness Publishing Limited
Hermes House
88-89 Blackfriars Road
London SE1 8HA

© Anness Publishing Limited 1999

Published in the USA by Lorenz Books
Anness Publishing Inc., 27 West 20th Street, New York, NY10011;
(800) 354-9657

This edition distributed in Canada by
Raincoast Books, 8680 Cambie Street, Vancouver, British Columbia V6P 6M9

ISBN 1 85967 887 4

All rights reserved. No part of this publication may be reproduced, stored in a retrieval system or transmitted in any way
or by any means, electronic, mechanical, photocopying, recording or otherwise, without the prior written
permission of the copyright holder.

A CIP catalogue record for this book is available from the British Library

*Publisher: Joanna Lorenz*
*Project editor: Simona Hill*
*Designer: Lilian Lindblom*
*Photographer: Tim Imrie*
*Stylist: Penny Boylan*
*Illustrators: Madeleine David and Lucinda Ganderton*

Printed and bound in Hong Kong/China

1 3 5 7 9 10 8 6 4 2

# CONTENTS

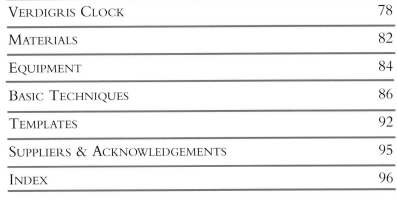

# INTRODUCTION

Self-hardening modelling clay is a modern development which has its roots in pottery. Although it cannot be worked by the traditional method on a wheel, it can be moulded, rolled, manipulated and cut just like real clay. This versatile medium has the qualities of its better-known counterpart, without the disadvantages. Real clay is messy and has to be fired before it can be finished, but self-hardening modelling clay can be cleared away quickly and left to dry in its own time. It has similarities too, to working with salt dough, since it does not require any specialist equipment or large working area set aside specifically for the task. Since this clay is available in white as well as traditional terracotta, colour can be added to the clay before it is shaped. Once dry, it can be decorated with anything from paint to gold leaf. No special glazes are required, just a couple of coats of varnish.

We have brought together 20 stunning projects for the home, ranging from a kitchen message board decorated with a three-dimensional hen, perfect for any country-style home, to opulent gilded tie-backs for lavish curtains and a textured lamp base with a quirky 1950s feel. Whether your style is to work on a large scale with a bright and cheerful colour scheme or for finely detailed, hand-crafted items in subtle tones, there is something here for everyone. If you feel daunted in any way, think back to the simple coil pots that you made as a child. How much fun it was, but also how simple! Have a go at the projects in this book and you will soon be hooked.

*Deborah Barker*

# FLOWER GARDEN CHALK BOARD

*Whether you want to jot down reminders for yourself or to leave important messages for somebody else, this little board in its pretty, rustic frame is perfect for the potting shed or to hang on the kitchen wall beside the back door.*

YOU WILL NEED
wooden fruit crate
saw
mitre block (square)
wood glue
staple gun
acrylic paints in a variety of colours
small household and medium artist's paintbrushes
glue gun
small chalk board with old frame removed
modelling clay
modelling tools
greaseproof (waxed) paper
tracing paper
paper
pencil
scissors
rolling pin
sharp knife

1 To make the rustic frame, remove the sides of the fruit crate and from it cut four lengths to fit the board dimensions. Mitre the corners or join the ends together. Use wood glue, then a staple gun, to hold the joints firmly. Using a household paintbrush, paint the front of the new frame bright green. Allow to dry, then glue the chalk board behind the frame.

2 To model a flower, roll six balls of clay the same size. Put one ball aside until step 3. Squeeze five of them into a point at one end. Using a rounded modelling tool, press each into a fat petal shape. Arrange the five petals into a flower shape.

3 Place the last ball in the flower centre and indent with a rounded modelling tool. For the fence, roll out and cut two strips each 1 cm/½ in wide to fit across the frame. Cut short strips for the posts. Trim the top of each post to a point. Construct the fence on greaseproof (waxed) paper.

4 For the leaves, roll out the clay, then cut basic leaf shapes and smooth out the edges with your fingers. Use a pointed modelling tool to trace a central vein on each one. Make 12 leaves in total.

5 Trace the templates provided for the pot and watering can and cut out. Cut out the shapes from clay, using the templates as a guide. Smooth the clay edges with your fingers.

6 For each three-dimensional pot, roll a ball of clay in your hand, then model it into a small pot shape. Let all the clay pieces dry on greaseproof paper for a few days.

7 Using an artist's paintbrush, paint the shapes in bright colours using acrylic paints, and allow to dry.

8 Use a glue gun to fix (attach) the picket fence and the other decorations to the chalk board frame.

# DECORATED FLOWERPOTS

*As terracotta pots age they acquire a beautiful patina of moss, algae and crystallized minerals,
but brand new machine-made pots can also be given a unique personality with
applied clay decorations. Here are some ideas*

YOU WILL NEED
stiff cardboard, tracing paper and pencil
craft knife and cutting mat
terracotta modelling clay
rolling pin
terracotta pots
masking tape
wood glue
contour paste for ceramics or similar relief outliner
talcum powder, if needed
sharp knife
cake decorating cutters: bow, leaves etc (optional)
3 mm/⅛ in rolling guides
tape measure
scrap paper
craft moulds (optional)
acrylic or emulsion (latex) paints (optional)
medium artist's and small household paintbrushes (optional)
matt acrylic varnish (optional)

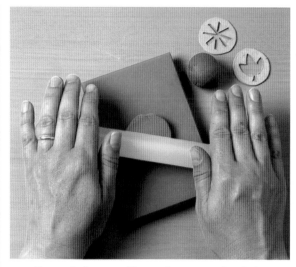

1 For each "wax seal" template, trace the design
provided on to stiff cardboard. Cut out the
central motif with a craft knife. Roll a small lump of
clay into a ball and flatten slightly.

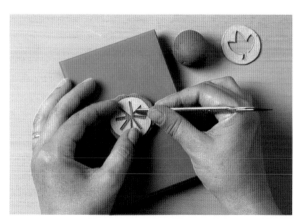

2 Firmly press the template into the clay, using the
blunt edge of a knife to help deepen the impression
through the holes. Carefully remove the template.

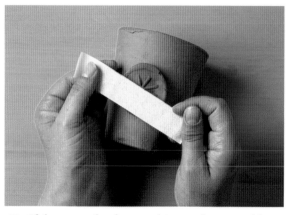

3 If the pot to be decorated is round, use masking
tape to attach the motif to the pot so that the
clay will dry with rounded sides.

▶

4 When the clay motif is completely dry, stick it firmly to the pot using wood glue.

5 For the square "seal", cut a piece of stiff cardboard to shape and decorate with contour paste, following the template or your own design. Allow to dry thoroughly.

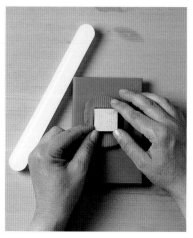

6 Roll out a small amount of clay. To stop the seal from sticking to the clay, dust the seal surface lightly with talcum powder. Press the seal into the clay. Remove carefully.

7 Cut around the motif with a sharp knife and tape to the pot to dry. Stick in place with wood glue.

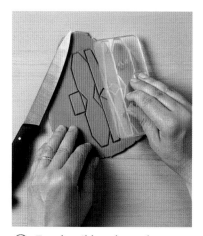

8 For the ribbon bow, draw a bow design freehand or use a cake decorating cutter. Roll out some clay to 3 mm/⅛ in thick. Press the cutter firmly into the clay, then remove the excess. Neaten any rough edges.

9 Fold the pieces into a bow shape and attach the "knot" piece by folding it over the front of the bow.

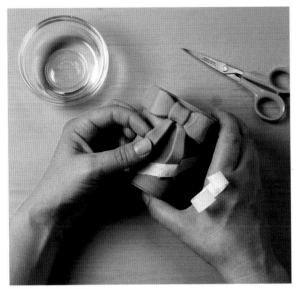

**10** Moisten the clay to stick the pieces together, then arrange the bow on the pot. Lift the ribbon ends slightly. Secure with masking tape until dry enough to glue in place.

**11** For the scalloped cuff, measure the circumference of the top of the pot then draw the cuff on paper to fit the pot.

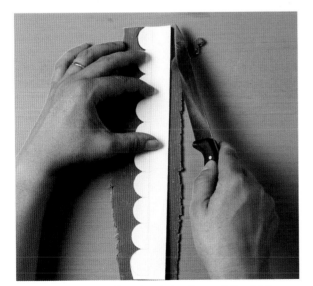

**12** Roll out a length of clay 3 mm/⅛in thick. Place the paper template on top and cut out with the sharp knife. Neaten any rough edges with the flat edge of a knife.

**13** Place the cuff around the rim of the pot. Moisten the edges to join them neatly. Work some clay over the join with your fingers to tidy it up and secure with masking tape. Allow to dry with the pot upside down. ▶

14 Craft moulds and cake decorating cutters can be used to make relief designs. Press clay into the mould, then cut out with a sharp knife, either cutting all around the detail or making it into a square or rectangular motif. You can combine several motifs on one pot.

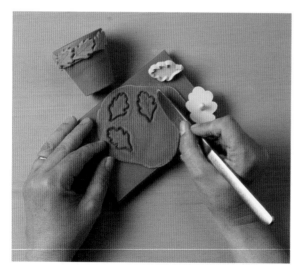

15 Some motifs, such as oak leaves or small daisies, look good when repeated. Paint the pots with acrylic paints, or for large areas, use emulsion (latex); terracotta is porous and will absorb a lot of paint. Protect with several coats of varnish.

# ROSE DRAWER HANDLES

*Beautiful, realistic-looking roses form the handles on a decorative set of small drawers in which to keep little treasures. The edges are painted to match the flowers, and the drawer fronts are given a charming crackle-glaze finish.*

YOU WILL NEED
paste food colouring or acrylic paints in pink and green
cocktail sticks (toothpicks)
white modelling clay
rolling pin
rose petal and calyx cake decorating cutters
plastic food wrap
balling tool (optional)
sharp knife
small wooden chest of drawers
fine sandpaper
acrylic primer or emulsion (latex) paint
artist's paintbrush
crackle-effect base coat
newspaper
crackle glaze in dark cream
masking tape
matt acrylic varnish
varnish brush
wood glue

1 Colour two balls of clay, one with pink and one with green food colouring or acrylic paints (see Basic Techniques). Add a small amount of colour to the clay, then fold the clay around the colour. Roll the clay between the palms of your hands into a sausage shape. Fold the ends to the middle and roll again. Repeat until all the colour is evenly distributed. The colour will alter as the clay dries.

2 To make the rose centre, roll a small cone in pink clay. Indent it at the wider end so that it will stand on its own small base. If you are making several roses, make them at the same time so that if you run out of coloured clay, they will all share the colour variations that may exist.

3 For the petals, roll out quite thinly a small amount of the pink clay. Take the small round cutter and press out two or three petals.

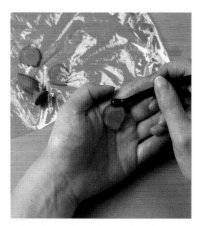

4 Pinch the edges of each petal between your finger and thumb to make them fine, or use a ball tool to shape the petals. Cover the petals not in use with polythene (plastic) to stop them drying out.

5 Moisten the cone and gently wrap a petal around it. Wrap the second petal opposite the first and overlapping it. Curl the edges back slightly with your fingers.

6 Cut out three or four medium-sized petals and cup them as before, curling the edges slightly before wrapping them around the flower. Open out the tops a little.

7 Cut out at least four larger petals and cup them slightly more than the previous petals. Fit them slightly lower than the previous layer and give them a more pronounced backward curl.

8 Use a sharp knife to trim away the stand made under the pink cone. Roll out thinly some green clay and cut out the calyx. Moisten the calyx and sit the rose inside it, arranging the calyx to curl very slightly away from the rose. Allow to dry thoroughly. ▶

9 To prepare the chest of drawers, sand any rough edges before applying a coat of primer or emulsion (latex) paint. Leave to dry thoroughly.

10 Spray the drawers with the crackle-effect base coat. Allow to dry for at least one hour. Spray with crackle glaze, following the manufacturer's instructions. Mask off each side as you work around the sides of the drawers to stop the paint spattering on finished work.

11 Paint the insides and edges of the drawers pink to match the colour of the roses. Allow to dry.

12 Apply several coats of matt acrylic varnish to the roses to help the clay harden. Stick the roses on to the drawers with wood glue.

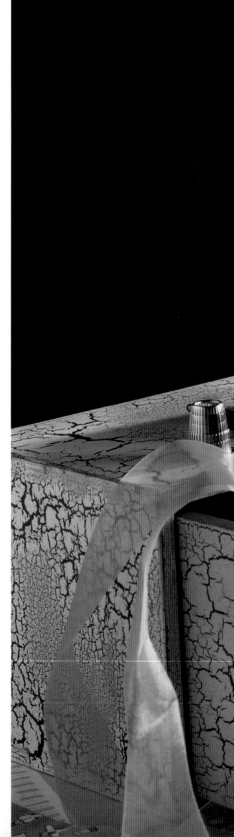

# GILDED CURTAIN TIE-BACKS

*These opulent golden tie-backs with an old-world feel will harmonize perfectly with the grandest curtains — no one would guess their humble origins as two plain wooden doorknobs and a ball of modelling clay.*

YOU WILL NEED
tracing paper and pencil for templates
powdered clay hardener
modelling clay
polythene (plastic) bag
3 mm/⅛ in rolling guides
rolling pin
large and small cup or glass to use as circular templates
sharp knife
modelling tool
scrap paper
PVA (white) glue
paintbrush
red oxide acrylic paint
wooden flat-topped doorknob
fine sandpaper
wood glue
acrylic gold size
Dutch metal leaf in gold
soft brush
acrylic gloss varnish

1 Mix the hardener into the clay (see Basic Techniques). Keep any clay not in use covered with a polythene (plastic) bag. To make the circular base for each tie-back, roll a piece of clay 3 mm/⅛ in thick and mark a circle with the large template. This will be the diameter of the finished tie-back. Cut out with a sharp knife. Smooth any fibrous edges.

2 Roll a piece of clay 1 cm/½ in thick. Use the small template to cut a circle. Position this on top of the first circle and place both on a sheet of paper on which you can leave the finished work to dry.

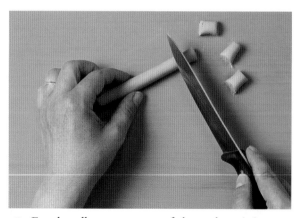

3 Evenly roll out a sausage of clay and cut it into sections with a sharp knife. Make all the pieces the same size.

4 Roll each piece into a ball sufficiently large to sit higher than the central circle when positioned on the large circle. Place each around the outside of the central circle, moistening the clay to help it stick. Indent each with the blunt side of the knife.

5 Make a second set of balls in the same way, this time rolling a slightly thinner sausage and cutting it into smaller sections. Place these around the edge of the small circle. These sit higher than the first row.

6 Roll some very thin sausages to position over the joins between the smaller clay balls. Arrange them in position and cut away the excess with the sharp knife. Tuck the ends through the gap between the balls as you work.

7 To make the centre, roll a ball of clay and flatten it slightly. Place this in the centre of the tie-back.

8 Make a tiny cone of clay to sit on the top of the flattened circle: pinch it with your fingers until you have the right shape. Moisten the clay and stick it on top.

9 Make a final set of smaller balls. Place these all around the central motif and score them with the blunt edge of the knife. Leave the clay to dry out completely.

10 Paint the tie-back with two coats of PVA (white) glue, so that everything adheres. When dry, paint all over with red oxide acrylic paint.

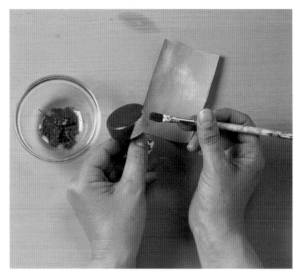

11 Rub down the doorknob with fine sandpaper, then paint it with red oxide. Apply several generous coats.

12 Stick the doorknob to the back of the tie-back with wood glue. Allow to dry.

13 Apply a coat of acrylic gold size over the tie-back. When the size is tacky, apply the Dutch metal leaf. Gently place a leaf over the clay and tap it down with a soft dry brush. Cover any bare areas only after the first layer has dried completely. Finish by applying four coats of acrylic gloss varnish.

# HEN MESSAGE BOARD

*This terracotta hen is constructed from layers of clay to give a three-dimensional effect.*
*Set against a simple background of unfinished, natural wood slats, it makes a lovely*
*wall decoration for a rustic-style kitchen.*

### YOU WILL NEED

pencil
scissors
3 mm/⅛ in rolling guides
rolling pin
terracotta modelling clay
sharp knife
modelling tool
rigid sheets of cardboard
masking tape
weight, if needed
wood glue
wooden fruit crate
screwdriver
saw
panel pins (thumbtacks)
hammer
picture hook (optional)
liquid clay hardener
paintbrushes
matt acrylic varnish
varnish brush
small hooks

1 Enlarge the templates provided to the required size. Make a template for each of the sections that build up into layers for the hen; number them if you find this helpful.

2 Roll out the clay to 3 mm/ ⅛ in thick. Place the first paper template on the clay and cut around the shape with a sharp knife. Repeat for each template.

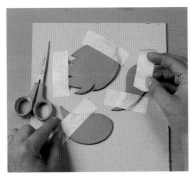

3 Smooth the edges of the three wing sections with a modelling tool to neaten them. Attach each piece to a rigid surface with masking tape to prevent the clay from distorting as it dries.

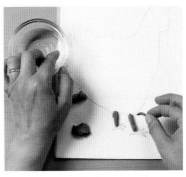

4 To make the legs, use the shape of the feet on the largest template as a guide. Form the legs and toes with sausage shapes. Carefully position each on the background template. Moisten the clay with water to make the legs stick.

▶

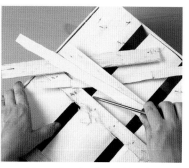

5 Model the details around the head and the comb using small pieces of clay. Moisten the clay to help it stick in place. Roll small sausages for the feathers around the legs. Use masking tape to secure the clay to a flat surface while drying and if necessary use a small weight to keep the body flat.

6 On the second body add an eye using a tiny ball. Model the beak from a small cone. Roll small sausages for the neck feathers. Arrange them in rows starting from the bottom and working upwards in layers. You may need to use a little glue at this stage. Use the point of the knife to align the feathers. Allow to dry thoroughly.

7 To make the board background, carefully dismantle the wooden crate using a screwdriver. Saw the wide slats to a uniform length for the background, then cut four more lengths to make a frame.

8 To construct the board, join the wide pieces with wood glue. Use masking tape to hold the board firm until it dries. Cut the frame pieces to size. Attach them to the background with panel pins (thumbtacks). Glue a hook on the back.

9 When the clay is dry, paint the pieces with liquid clay hardener, then follow with several coats of matt acrylic varnish.

10 Carefully assemble the hen in layers, sticking the pieces firmly together with wood glue. Attach small hooks around the frame to finish.

# SUMMER VASE

*To give a room an instant splash of Mediterranean sunshine, transform a plain ceramic vase*
*with bright yellow enamel paint and a boldly painted relief design of lavender sprigs —*
*the essence of Provence.*

YOU WILL NEED
ceramic vase
quick-drying yellow enamel paint
medium and fine paintbrushes
modelling clay
pointed modelling tool
acrylic paints in green and lavender
clear enamel spray

1 Wash and dry the vase to remove grease and dust. Apply a coat of yellow enamel paint and allow to dry. Paint on another coat if necessary to achieve an even coverage.

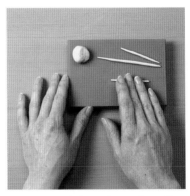

2 For each lavender sprig, roll a small ball of clay into one long thin sausage and two shorter ones; these will form the stem and leaves.

3 Using a paintbrush, apply a wide stripe of yellow enamel paint where you intend to put a lavender sprig. This glues the clay in place while it dries.

4 Carefully press the stalk into position on the vase.

5 Flatten the smaller sausages to resemble long thin leaves and position them on each side of the stem, close to the base. To make each flower, roll a tiny piece of clay into a ball. Press each tiny ball to the top of the flower stem.

6 Using a pointed modelling tool, make an indentation in the base of each flower. Make several flower stems in this way and place them at random all over the vase. Set aside overnight for the clay to dry completely.

7 Using acrylic paints and a fine paintbrush, colour the lavender sprigs and leave to dry.

8 Protect the finished vase with a coat of clear enamel spray.

# BACCHUS GARDEN PLAQUE

*Set a convivial tone for summer parties in the garden by hanging
this terracotta relief on the wall. The genial god of wine can smile benignly
down on the proceedings.*

YOU WILL NEED
pencil
tracing paper
scissors
5 mm/¼ in rolling guides
rolling pin
modelling clay
sharp knife
hatpin or tapestry needle
modelling tools
5 cm/2 in strong wire
wire cutters
acrylic craft paints in red oxide and cream
medium artist's paintbrushes
spray matt varnish

1 Enlarge the template provided to 25 cm/10 in
wide at its widest point. Trace the outline and
details and cut out. Roll out a slab of clay the same
size as the template and 5 mm/¼ in thick. Place the
tracing on the clay and cut around it.

2 Use a hatpin to transfer the details on to the clay,
by making a series of pinpricks along each line.
Peel off the paper and smooth the edges.

3 Draw in the features with a pointed modelling tool, using the pin pricks as a guide.

4 Make the hair from small sausages and coils of clay pressed gently along the guidelines. Use a flat-ended modelling tool to emphasize the shapes between the curls.

5 Roll out the remaining clay to a thickness of 5 mm/¼ in. Transfer the leaves from the tracing. Cut them out and press into place on the guidelines. Use a modelling tool to make the veins in the leaves.

6 Make small balls for the grapes and press into place, moistening the clay if necessary to help it stick. Make the beard in the same way as the hair, with coils and spirals of clay.

7 Press a loop of wire into the back to make a hanger for the plaque, then leave the plaque to dry completely.

8 Combine red oxide and cream paint to make a deep terracotta shade. Paint the plaque and allow it to dry thoroughly.

9 For a more weathered, textured effect, add another coat of red oxide paint, applied with a dry brush to give a stippled result.

10 Add some highlights with a little cream paint, stippled on to the hair and beard with a dry brush. Spray on several coats of matt varnish to make the plaque weatherproof.

# SILVER-LEAF FINIALS

*Give a plain wooden curtain pole a flourish at each end. These silvered finials look like*
*intricate carved wood and make a beautiful finishing touch at the window.*
*The pole and fittings can be decorated in silver to match.*

### YOU WILL NEED

| | |
|---|---|
| bradawl | modelling tools |
| 2 small metal screwtop lids | tracing paper and pencil |
| wood glue | scissors |
| 2 small wood screws | sharp knife |
| 2 x 7.5 cm/3 in lengths of | turquoise acrylic or |
| wooden dowel, each | emulsion (latex) paint |
| 1 cm/½ in diameter | paintbrushes |
| screwdriver | curtain pole and fittings |
| stiff cardboard | acrylic size |
| craft knife | stencil brush |
| metal ruler | Dutch metal leaf in silver |
| cutting mat | soft brush |
| tinfoil | spray acrylic varnish |
| modelling clay | epoxy resin glue |

1 Pierce a small hole through the centre of each
screwtop with a bradawl. Using wood glue and a
small wood screw, attach each screwtop lid to a
length of dowel. Allow the glue to set hard.

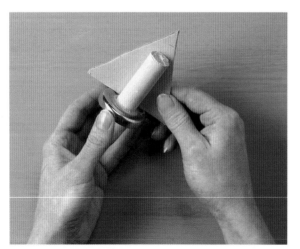

2 Cut a triangle for each finial from stiff cardboard
and glue to the back of each dowel.

3 Take a piece of tinfoil, crumple it a little and
then wrap it around the dowel and the cardboard
to make a smooth shape.

4 Break off small pieces of modelling clay and cover the entire shape with a thin layer. Use your fingers or a flat modelling tool to smooth out the surface of the clay. Repeat for the second finial.

5 Roll small balls of clay in the palm of your hand. Press each one lightly to the top of the pointed shape in close overlapping rows. Use a pointed modelling tool to make an indentation in the base of each one.

6 Trace and enlarge the leaf template provided. Cut out three leaves from a flattened piece of clay for each finial.

7 Wrap the leaves around the berry-covered centre piece and press the base of each securely on to the clay. Curl the tip of each leaf outwards. Repeat for the second finial.

8 Using a pointed modelling tool, lightly trace the veins on each leaf into the surface of the clay.

9 Roll two small balls of clay into a tapered sausage. Roll up the tapered end and press the other end to the base of the finial. Use modelling tools to smooth out any unsightly joins at the base. Leave the finials to dry for a few days.

10 Apply one or two coats of turquoise acrylic or emulsion (latex) paint to the finials, the curtain pole and fittings. Allow to dry thoroughly after each coat.

11 Apply a mottled coat of acrylic size using a stencil brush. Leave to become slightly tacky.

12 Apply the silver leaf one sheet at a time, tapping down gently with a soft dry brush. Make sure that there are no draughts in your work space as the leaf is very light and delicate and will blow away. The leaf will adhere unevenly allowing the coloured paint to show through.

13 With the same dry brush, gently remove all loose flakes of leaf. Brush the surface firmly to make sure that the silver leaf has adhered. Seal all surfaces with one or two coats of varnish and allow to dry completely. Glue the finials to the ends of the curtain pole with epoxy resin glue.

# GEOMETRIC PICTURE FRAMES

*These pure white frames are co-ordinated yet individually decorated. Restrained,*
*geometric relief designs add interest with the play of light and shadow,*
*yet do not overwhelm the contents of the frames.*

YOU WILL NEED
3 mm/⅛ in rolling guides
rolling pin
white modelling clay
small round and square metal cutters (cookie cutters)
cocktail stick (toothpick)
sharp knife and ruler, if necessary
round-ended knife
masking tape
plain wooden picture frames
fine sandpaper
white acrylic or emulsion (latex) paint
paintbrush
emery board
wood glue
matt acrylic varnish

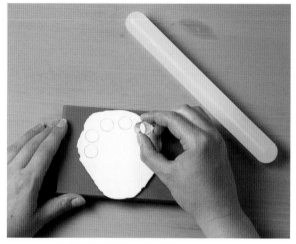

1 Roll out a small piece of clay to an even
thickness of about 3 mm/⅛ in. Using the round
cutter, cut out several shapes from the clay.

2 Pierce the centre of each clay disc with a cocktail
stick (toothpick) and allow to dry.

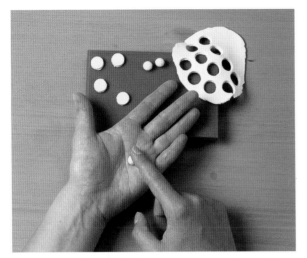

3 For an alternate design, cut out a number of clay discs as before. Roll each disc in the palm of your hand, then between your fingers to make more spherical, evenly sized balls. Allow the balls to dry thoroughly.

4 For the squares, roll out the clay, then cut out small squares using a square cutter. (Use a sharp knife with a ruler as a guide if you do not have a cutter.) Decorate with several different marks: single holes, straight lines, using the flat end of a knife, and a combination of both. Aim to have about five different designs. Adhere each to a flat surface with masking tape so that the edges do not curl. Allow to dry.

5 To prepare the frames, first sand each gently to provide a key for the paint, then apply several coats of white acrylic or emulsion (latex) paint.

6 File any rough edges from the clay motifs using an emery board. Arrange the motifs on the frames, experimenting with different combinations until you are satisfied. Stick in place with wood glue. ▶

7 When the glue is dry, apply one or two coats of white paint to the entire frame, followed by several coats of matt acrylic varnish. Allow each coat to dry before applying the next.

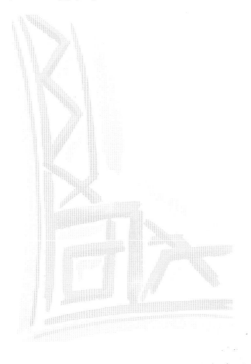

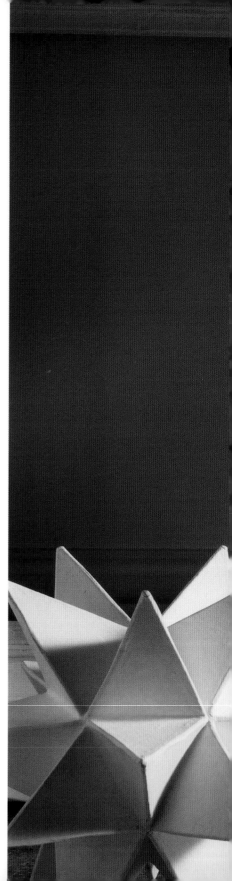

# LEAF WALL PLAQUES

*Achieve a lovely three-dimensional effect by impressing a simple cardboard template
in a flat slab of soft clay. The cut-out details are given depth by hidden spacers that hold
each plaque away from the wall.*

YOU WILL NEED

| | |
|---|---|
| tracing paper and pencil | scissors |
| cardboard for template | fine wire |
| craft knife | wire cutters |
| cutting mat | wood glue |
| hardener (optional) | emery board or fine sandpaper |
| modelling clay | PVA (white) glue |
| 1 cm/½ in rolling guides | paintbrush |
| rolling pin | acrylic paints |
| sharp knife | matt acrylic varnish |
| paper | |

1 Using the template provided, cut a leaf design
from cardboard. Mix the clay hardener into
the clay. Using rolling guides, roll out a slab of clay
to a depth of about 1 cm/½ in. Position the template
on the clay and press it gently and evenly down so
that clay protrudes through the holes. Use the knife
to help.

2 Remove the template. Make a paper template for
the plaque shape. Place it very lightly on the clay,
and cut out the plaque using a sharp knife.

3 Carefully cut out the leaf veins from the clay.
Smooth the edges of the plaque with the flat
edge of the knife. Allow the clay to dry completely.

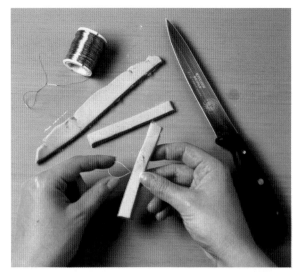

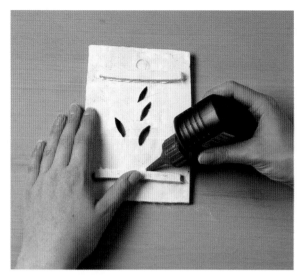

4 Roll out two lengths of clay for backing strips. Cut a short piece of wire and insert it into the top of one strip, taking care to arrange the loop so that it will not be seen when the plaque is hanging. If you are making a set of plaques, make sure all the wires are an equal length.

5 When the plaque and strips are dry, stick the strips to the back of the plaque using wood glue. One strip should be across the top of the plaque, and another across the bottom.

6 File or sand the edges of the clay very gently to remove burrs. Paint the entire plaque with two coats of PVA (white) glue to seal the clay and help prevent chipping.

7 Add a coat of acrylic paint. Then paint the indented leaf a slightly darker shade of the main colour. Seal with several coats of matt acrylic varnish, allowing it to dry between coats.

# FLORAL LINEN SCENTERS

*Because clay is porous it can be scented with your favourite essential oil and it will hold the perfume beautifully for weeks. These pretty floral motifs will keep your own clothes smelling sweet; they also make superb presents.*

YOU WILL NEED

tracing paper and pencil
scissors
3 mm/⅛ in rolling guides
rolling pin
modelling clay
sharp knife
modelling tool
essential oil
wire cutters
wire coathanger
pliers

rigid sheet of cardboard
masking tape
small flower cutters (for cake decorating)
cocktail stick (toothpick)
fine wire
wood glue
jam jar
acrylic gouache
paintbrush
matt acrylic varnish
ribbon

1 Enlarge the template provided to the required size and cut out. Roll out the clay evenly, to a depth of about 3 mm/⅛ in. Place the template on the clay and cut around the shape with a sharp knife.

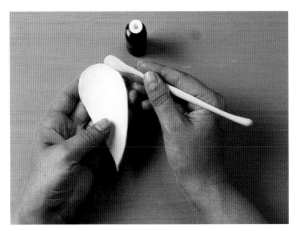

2 Tidy the edges of the clay with the modelling tool. Sprinkle on a few drops of essential oil.

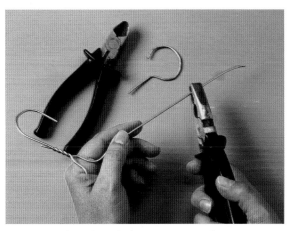

3 Cut a short length from a wire coathanger, using wire cutters. Shape with pliers into a neat hook. ▶

45

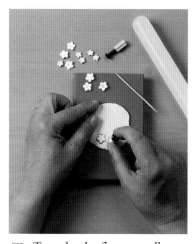

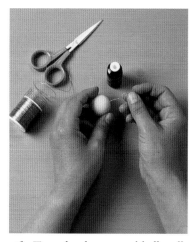

4 Gently push at least 2.5 cm/ 1 in of the hook into the top of the clay. Secure on a rigid surface with masking tape to keep the clay flat, and allow to dry.

5 To make the flowers, roll out a thin piece of clay. Using a flower cutter, cut out the required number of flowers. Carefully pierce the centres with a cocktail stick (toothpick). Allow to dry.

6 To make the scented ball, roll a piece of clay into a sphere in the palm of your hand. Insert a very small loop of fine wire deep into the clay. Sprinkle with essential oil. Allow to dry.

7 Stick the flowers to the motifs using wood glue. Work around the ball in sections. Suspend the ball by the wire loop from a cocktail stick over a jar to dry. Add more essential oil as desired.

8 When the flowers are dry, check that the hook is firmly in place: use glue to secure it if necessary. Paint the motifs with acrylic gouache, dabbing the paint into the crevices. Begin with a dark shade, then brush a lighter shade on to the raised surfaces with a dry brush. Apply a coat of matt acrylic varnish.

9 To cover the hook with ribbon, leave an end to tie in a bow and work up the hook from the motif to the cut end of wire, then back again. Finish by tying the ends of the ribbon in a bow. Refresh the clay from time to time with essential oil, but make sure it is dry before hanging it next to clothing.

# MOSAIC MIRROR

*The organic, freeform shape of this mirror frame is inspired by the pliable nature of the clay, but enlivened by the sharp contrast of angular shards of glossy tiles and opalescent beads embedded into the clay while it is still soft.*

YOU WILL NEED
assorted ceramic tiles
2 mirror tiles each 15 cm/6 in square
old towel
hammer
scissors
1 cm/½ in and 8 mm/⅜ in rolling guides
rolling pin
modelling clay
sharp knife
fruit corer
wire for hanging
8 beads
fine sandpaper
acrylic gesso
pink acrylic paint
paintbrushes

1 Wrap the ceramic tiles and one of the mirror tiles in an old towel. Hit with a hammer to break the tiles randomly into mosaic pieces.

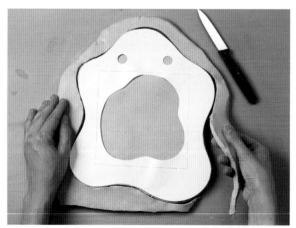

2 Enlarge the frame template provided and cut out. Cut out the hanging holes and central opening. Roll out a piece of clay 1 cm/½ in thick for the mirror back. Place the template on top and cut around it. Pull away the excess clay.

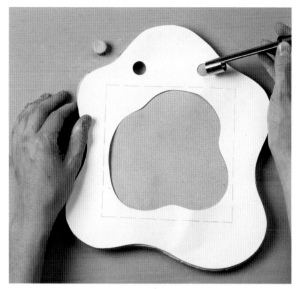

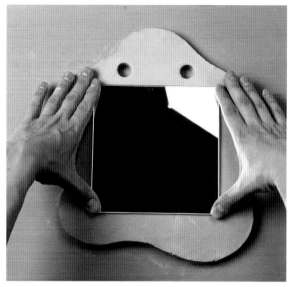

3 Punch out the hanging holes using a fruit corer. Do not cut away the clay in the centre of the mirror. Remove the template.

4 Position the remaining mirror tile on the clay using the broken lines on the template as a guide. Press the mirror into the clay. Thread the hanging wire through the holes and secure at the back. Press the clay over the wire at the front.

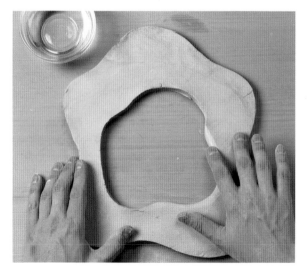

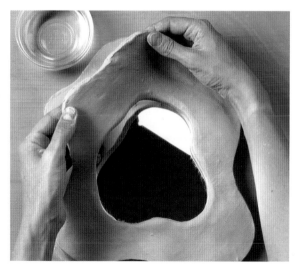

5 Roll a second piece of clay 8 mm/⅜ in thick for the front of the frame. Place the template on top and cut around the circumference and the central opening. Pull away the excess clay. Smooth the edges of the opening with a moistened finger.

6 Carefully lift the clay front and place it over the mirror tile and the back, matching the outer edges. Smooth the outer edges with a moistened finger to blend the seam and the cut edges.

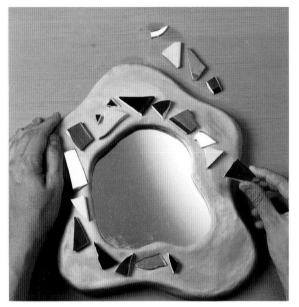

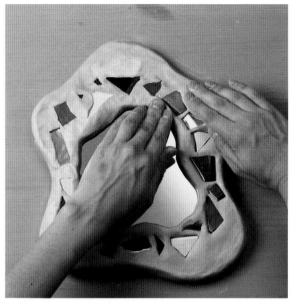

7 Moisten the top of the clay. Arrange the mosaic pieces around the mirror.

8 Press the mosaic pieces into the clay. Then press the clay over the edges of the pieces to secure.

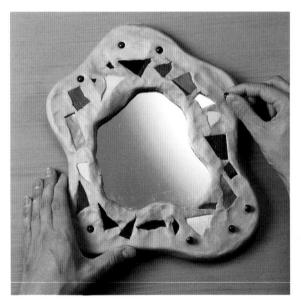

9 Arrange the beads on the frame, then embed them into the clay. Leave the mirror to harden completely. If any cracks appear in the clay around the mosaic pieces, add more moistened clay and leave to harden.

10 Lightly sand the outer edges. Undercoat the mirror with acrylic gesso. Paint the clay frame pink. Use a fine brush to paint around the edges of the mirror tile, the mosaic pieces and beads.

# TEXTURED LAMP BASE

*The gourd-like shape and surface texture of this lamp base are achieved*
*by pressing small pieces of rolled clay onto a papier-mâché and wire armature.*
*The sponged painting technique accentuates its tactile quality.*

YOU WILL NEED
long-nosed pliers
chicken wire
tape measure
short length of 2.5 cm/1 in diameter dowel
medium- and fine-gauge galvanized wire
newspaper
wallpaper paste
modelling clay
rolling pin
acrylic paints in cream, yellow, orange and red
paintbrush
natural sponge
bottle lamp fitting and flex (cord)

1 Using pliers, cut a rectangle of chicken wire
about 15 x 19 cm/6 x 7½ in. Turn in one long
edge for extra strength. Roll the short end around a
length of dowel to form a cylinder for the neck.

2 Cut another rectangle of chicken wire about
30 x 45 cm/12 x 18 in and bend it to form a
cylinder, twisting the ends of the wire together
to make a neat seam. Use the pliers to pinch the
chicken wire together a little at one end: this will
form the bottom edge of the lamp base.

3 Bend a length of medium-gauge galvanized wire
into a circle about 10 cm/4 in in diameter, and
bind with fine-gauge wire all the way around.

4 Place the wire ring inside the bottom of the cylinder, fold the ends of the chicken wire over the ring and, using the fine wire, "stitch" the ring securely in place.

5 Use the pliers to pinch the chicken wire, working slowly, row by row, to make the cylinder into a smooth pear shape.

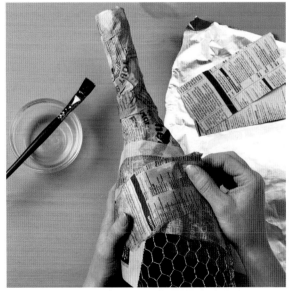

6 Slide the neck piece into the top of the wire shape and bind in place with fine-gauge galvanized wire, as before.

7 Cover the wire armature with strips of newspaper soaked in wallpaper paste to make a smoother surface. Leave for a few days to dry hard. ▶

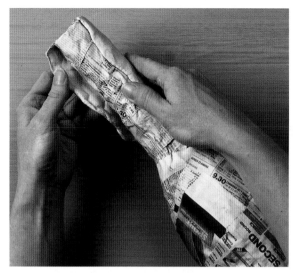

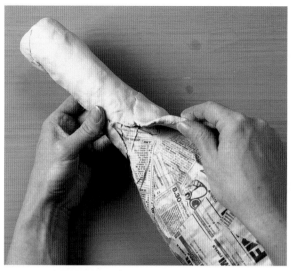

8 Cover the dry armature with clay, beginning at the neck. Roll out slabs of clay to a thickness of about 1 cm/½ in. Place each on the armature, smoothing out the joins (seams) with your fingers.

9 Work your way down the armature, adding rolled-out sections of clay until it is completely covered. Pierce a hole near the base for the flex (cord). Leave the lamp base to dry out completely.

10 Paint the top half of the lamp base with one or two coats of cream acrylic paint, allowing each coat to dry before applying the next. Using a small natural sponge, apply a mottled band of yellow paint, blending to orange lower down. Apply a mottled band of red paint blending to a solid colour at the bottom.

11 Put the flex (cord) through the top of the lamp base and out through the hole at the bottom, then push the lamp fitting into the neck. It should fit quite snugly, but if necessary, use a little clay to fill in any gaps.

# ROCOCO WALL PLAQUE

*A rough-cast plaster finish enlivens a plain interior wall but you can add more texture*
*and decorative interest by applying clay motifs directly to the wall before painting it.*
*Highlight the details with white as a finishing touch.*

**YOU WILL NEED**
tracing paper and pencil
scissors
masking tape
permanent marker pen
8 mm/⅜ in and 5 mm/¼ in rolling guides
rolling pin
modelling clay
sharp knife
wood glue
fine and medium paintbrushes
fruit corer
drinking straw
blue emulsion (latex) paint
white emulsion paint
PVA (white) glue

1 Enlarge the templates provided for the motifs to a suitable size. Cut each out of paper. Tape the plaque template B to a coarsely plastered wall and draw carefully around the outline with a permanent marker pen. Remove the template then draw around motifs A in the same way.

2 Roll the clay out to a thickness of 8 mm/⅜ in. Cut out motif A using a sharp knife. Smooth the cut edges with the flat edge of a knife.

3 On the wall, spread wood glue inside motif A and up to the drawn lines.

4 Carefully press the clay motif A on to the wall over the drawn motif. Smooth along the edges with a moistened finger.

5 Roll out another piece of clay to a thickness of 5 mm/¼ in. Cut out the relief pieces for motif A. Moisten the undersides and press in position. Pat the cut edges with a moistened finger to round them.

6 Indent the details on the clay using the handle of a fine paintbrush.

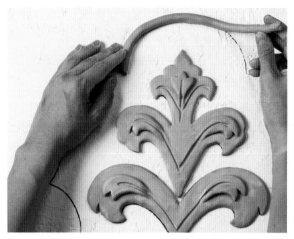

7 Roll sausages of clay 1 cm/½ in thick. Apply a line of glue to the wall along one section of the plaque outline. Press the sausage on top. Cut off the excess clay at the angled points. Repeat until the plaque outline is complete.

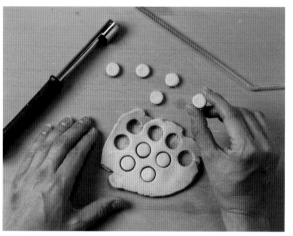

8 Roll out some clay to a thickness of 5 mm/¼ in. Stamp nine circles using a fruit corer. Gently roll each circle between your fingers to smooth the sides. Indent the centres of all the circles using a drinking straw. Dab a little glue on the underside of each and press three circles to the wall below the point of motif B. Press the remaining circles to the plaque outline at the corners.

9 Roll six 1.5 cm/⅝ in diameter balls of clay for the leaves. Mould each ball between your fingers to form a flattened leaf shape. Indent a vein along the centre with the handle of a fine paintbrush. Dab wood glue on the undersides and press each leaf on to the plaque outline.

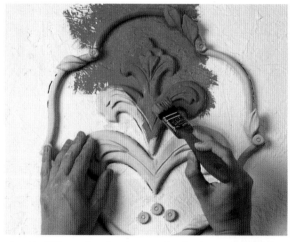

10 When the clay is completely dry, paint the plaque with PVA (white) glue followed when dry by two coats of blue emulsion (latex) paint. To finish, pick out the plaque details in white emulsion paint as desired.

# FLORENTINE BOXES

*Formalized leaves and gilded scroll-work turn simple square boxes into encrusted Renaissance treasures. You could line the inside of each with sumptuous fabric to hold jewellery or mementoes, or to display a very special gift.*

YOU WILL NEED
square and rectangular cardboard craft boxes
tracing paper
hard and soft pencils
masking tape
ball-point pen
modelling clay
modelling tools
PVA (white) glue
medium and fine paintbrushes
acrylic craft paints in white, pale lilac and pale blue
dark and pale gold metallic paint
matt acrylic spray varnish

1 Enlarge the templates provided to fit the top and sides of the box lid. Trace the outline with a hard pencil, then rub over the reverse with a soft pencil. Tape the paper to the lid. Draw over the lines again using a ball-point pen.

2 Make the four leaf shapes from small rolls of clay and press them into position on the box lid. Use modelling tools to add the details, and smooth the clay with a damp finger.

3 Make the dots from small balls of clay. Press them in place with the point of a pencil.

4 Finish the design on top of the lid by adding the four trefoil motifs on the corners.

5 Make the scrolls and leaves for each side of the lid. Allow the clay to dry thoroughly.

6 Paint the lid with PVA (white) glue diluted with an equal quantity of water. Paint the lid and box with white acrylic paint.

7 Paint the lid with a base coat of pale lilac.

8 Add a stippling of pale blue paint, applied with an almost dry brush.

9 Using a fine brush, paint the motifs in dark gold. When dry, add pale gold highlights as desired.

10 Give a textured look to the lid by brushing over the surface with a dry brush loaded with a small amount of gold paint.

11 Paint the bottom of the box to match, adding a small amount of gold paint to each edge. Finish by spraying the box and lid with a protective coat of matt varnish.

# MEXICAN CANDLESTICKS

*Bright, hot colours give a carnival feel to these pretty candlesticks shaped like exotic*
*desert flowers. The base of each is simply made from balls of clay stacked on top of each other,*
*taking care to keep the sticks straight while they dry.*

YOU WILL NEED
rolling pin
modelling clay
7.5 cm/3 in diameter glass
sharp knife
modelling tool
cocktail sticks (toothpicks)
candles
knitting needle
acrylic craft paints in pink, green, light and dark blue
paintbrushes
acrylic matt varnish

1 For each candlestick, roll out a piece of clay to a
thickness of about 5 mm/¼ in. Use the rim of the
glass to stamp a circle on it.

2 Cut out the disc using a
sharp knife and neaten the
edges using a modelling tool.

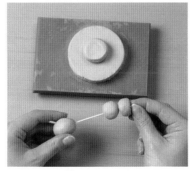

3 Press a 3 cm/1¼ in diameter
ball of clay into the centre of
the disc and flatten. Make a flattened 2 cm/¾ in ball, a 3 cm/1¼ in
ball and an elongated 4 cm/1½ in
ball, and thread them all on to a
cocktail stick (toothpick). Press into
the middle of the base.

4 Hollow out a ball of clay to
fit the candle. To make small
petals, roll out pea-sized balls of
clay and flatten them. Press each
to the rim of the candlestick cup
for the decoration.

▶

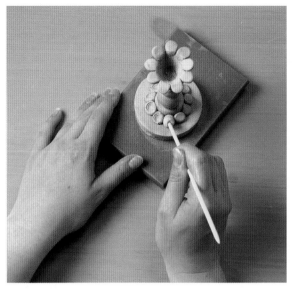

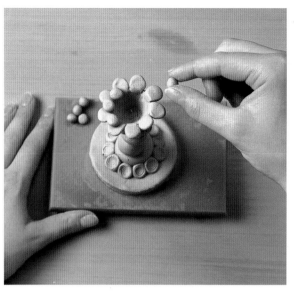

5 Make small balls of clay and press them in a ring around the base of the candlestick. Indent each with the top of a knitting needle.

6 Roll some more small balls to decorate the rim of the candlestick and the section between the cup and stem of the candlestick. Indent each with the point of the knitting needle.

7 Score a series of lines on the base, cup and elongated clay ball using a cocktail stick. Allow the candlestick to dry completely.

8 Paint the top petals and the round ball pink, the rings of dots green and the rest of the candlestick pale blue. Drag dark blue paint over the scored stripes for a two-colour effect. Individualize the candlestick as desired. Finish with several coats of matt varnish.

# COIL POT

*Long before the invention of the potter's wheel, craftsmen used to create vessels of great beauty and elegance, using this ancient coiling technique. It is still used by potters all over the world.*

YOU WILL NEED
powdered clay hardener
modelling clay
polythene (plastic) bag
rolling pin
6 mm/¼ in rolling guides
cup or glass
sharp knife
modelling tool
PVA (white) glue
coarse and fine paintbrushes
water-based household paints in deep
powder blue, aqua and lime
scarlet acrylic gouache
matt acrylic varnish

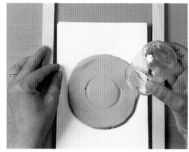

1 Mix the hardener into the clay. Keep any clay not in use covered with a polythene (plastic) bag. To make the base of the bowl, roll out a circle of clay between rolling guides. Gently press a cup or glass into the clay to mark a circle the size you wish the base of the pot to be.

2 Roll a small piece of clay into a sausage. Keep the sausage as even as possible. The diameter of the coil will determine the thickness of the pot walls throughout the process.

3 Arrange the sausage over the indented base mark. Cut the ends at an angle to overlap them neatly. Smooth the join (seam) in the coil using a modelling tool.

4 The first coil must adhere to the base, so smooth the clay on to the base all around the inside of the coil, using your finger or the modelling tool.

5 Score the top of the first coil lightly with the tip of the sharp knife to help the next layer to adhere.

6 Make a second coil in the same way. Place it on top of the first, making sure the join is in a different place from that of the first coil.

7 Using the modelling tool, smooth the coils together inside and outside as you make the pot walls. The modelling tool helps create texture, so experiment with different score-marks until you find one that suits the piece you are making.

8 As the pot gets taller, position each coil slightly to the edge of the one below to make the opening larger.

9 Cut away the excess clay around the base of the pot with the sharp knife. When you have finished the pot, smooth the top edge with the sharp knife or modelling tool. Allow the pot to dry completely.

10 Seal the pot with PVA (white) glue, diluted with an equal quantity of water. Using a large, coarse brush, paint the outside of the pot with two or three shades of colour, brushing the paint on at random and build-ing up the layers of colour. Keep the brush quite dry so that the paint picks up the texture made with the modelling tool.

11 Paint the inside with a single colour to complement the outside. Finish by painting around the rim with scarlet acrylic gouache, or the bright shade of your choice. Varnish the pot with several coats of matt acrylic varnish.

# STONE-EFFECT PLATTERS

*These square dishes, each gently curved and raised by simple feet, have an exquisitely restrained, Japanese quality. They eschew fussy decoration, but their style is enhanced by the wonderful surface texture, reminiscent of finely-worked stone.*

### YOU WILL NEED

soft, porous cloth
plastic food container
polythene (plastic) bag
elastic band
powdered clay hardener
modelling clay
rolling pin
5 mm/¼ in rolling guides
hessian (burlap)
paper
scissors
ruler
sharp knife
masking tape
PVA (white) glue
medium artist's
paintbrush
emery board or fine sandpaper
fine sand
acrylic paints
acrylic matt varnish

1 To prepare the mould, stretch the soft, porous cloth over the top of the container and secure it with an elastic band. Make sure the fabric is not too taut, as you want to create a gentle curve to mould the clay into a dish shape.

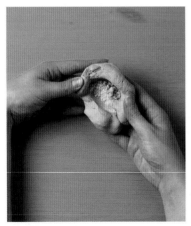

2 Knead the hardener into the clay. Keep any clay not in use in a polythene (plastic) bag.

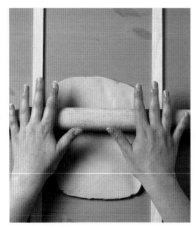

3 Roll out a slab of clay to an even thickness of 5 mm/¼ in, using rolling guides.

4 Place the hessian (burlap) on top and roll over it to make an impression in the clay.

5 Make a square template, measuring 12 cm/4½ in. (For a large platter, make a 12 x 20 cm/4½ x 8 in template). Using the template, cut out the clay with a sharp knife.

6 Place the square carefully in the cloth mould and allow to dry thoroughly. This will give the clay a slightly scooped shape.

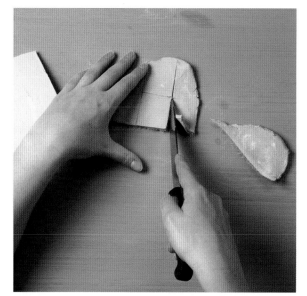

7 To make a foot for the dish, roll out a piece of clay to about 5 mm/¼ in thick. Cut it into a 5 cm/2 in square using a sharp knife.

8 Place the foot on the underside of the dried dish and secure with masking tape. When dry, stick the foot in place with undiluted PVA (white) glue. ▶

9 File the raw edges of the platter to achieve a slightly rounded edge.

10 Paint the platter with two coats of PVA glue. While the second coat is still wet, sprinkle with fine sand. Allow the glue to dry before shaking off the excess sand. Repeat for a more textured look.

11 To coat the sides, paint with PVA glue, then dip into the sand and allow to dry before working on the underside. When you have achieved the desired effect, coat the whole platter with PVA.

12 Mix acrylic paint to a sandy stone colour and paint the platter all over, adding more coats until the desired shade is reached. Seal with at least two coats of acrylic matt varnish.

# FLEUR-DE-LYS WASTEBASKET

*Emblazoned with elegant heraldic motifs, this pretty yet functional object is perfect
in a formal room. Painting it with a subtle mix of colours will give it an appearance of
antique metal, and enhance the relief effect of the clay decorations.*

YOU WILL NEED
pencil
thin cardboard for template
scissors
5 mm/¼ in rolling guides
rolling pin
modelling clay
sharp knife
modelling tools
ruler
medium-density fibreboard (MDF) wastebasket
glue gun
acrylic paints in silver, dark grey, brown and cream
small household and medium
artist's paintbrushes
small sponge
spray matt varnish

1 Enlarge the template provided to 12.5 cm/5 in
across. Transfer the outline on to thin cardboard
and cut out. Roll out the clay to 5 mm/¼ in thick –
you will need enough to make four fleurs-de-lys.
Place the template on the clay and cut around the
outside edge with a sharp knife.

2 Peel off the template and tidy the edges of the
clay with a flat modelling tool or your finger.

3 Draw in the markings with a modelling tool, then allow the shapes to dry.

4 Draw two diagonals and a central vertical line on each side of the wastebasket.

5 Use the glue gun to glue the clay shapes carefully in place, making sure that they all line up. Keep your fingers away from the hot glue.

6 Paint the wastebasket and the fleur-de-lys motifs with silver paint. Allow to dry.

7 Sponge on a thin layer of dark grey to look like galvanized metal.

8 Add some touches of brown paint, emphasizing the relief areas of the motifs.

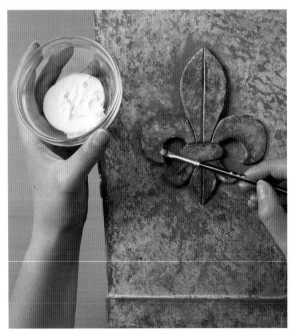

9 With a dry brush, add small areas of cream paint to the motifs and wastebasket.

10 Finish off with several coats of spray matt varnish to protect the paintwork and motifs.

# VERDIGRIS CLOCK

*This delightful floral clock has no need of numerals: the twelve petals show the hours instead. The verdigris effect is achieved with clever use of paint, a technique which emphasizes the solidity of the sculpted design.*

YOU WILL NEED
tracing paper
pencil
scissors
5 mm/¼ in rolling guides
rolling pin
modelling clay
sharp knife
hatpin or tapestry needle
modelling tools
ruler
clock mechanism with 7.5 cm/3 in hands
5 cm/2 in length of strong wire
glue gun
acrylic craft paints in bronze, mid-green, pale green and cream
medium and small artist's paintbrushes
varnish

1 Enlarge the template provided to measure 23 cm/9 in across and draw the outside petals and the inner circle separately on tracing paper. Cut out. Roll out a slab of clay 5 mm/¼ in thick, slightly larger than the main clock piece. Place the template on the clay. Cut out around the edge with a sharp knife.

2 Transfer the markings by pricking through the paper with a hatpin, then peel off the paper.

3 Use a flat modelling tool to emphasize these outlines and to give a three-dimensional shape to the petals. Smooth the clay as necessary.

4 Cut a square from the centre of the circle that is 1 cm/⅜ in larger all around than the clock mechanism. Attach a hanging loop of wire to the back of the top petal.

5 Roll out a 15 cm/6 in diameter disc of clay for the clock centre. Cut out and transfer the markings to the clay as before, using the template.

6 Make a hole in the centre to fit the clock spindle, then shape around the dots and petals with a modelling tool to give a three-dimensional look.

7 Allow both pieces to dry completely, then glue them together with a glue gun.

8 Paint the entire piece with a base coat of bronze acrylic craft paint. Allow to dry.

9 Brush on a coat of mid-green paint, allowing some of the bronze to show through.

10 Stipple on layers of pale green and cream with a dry brush. Paint with varnish to protect the surface.

11 Attach the clock mechanism, making sure that at 12.00 the hands line up with the wire hanger on the back of the finished piece.

# MATERIALS

ACRYLIC VARNISH
This comes in matt, satin and gloss finishes, in liquid or aerosol form.

CLAY HARDENERS
Powdered hardeners harden the clay throughout; liquid hardeners seal and harden the outside only.

DUTCH METAL LEAF
Apply metal leaf for decoration.

GLUE
Use strong woodworking glue to stick clay to other surfaces and for repairs. Dilute PVA (white) glue with water for use as a sealant, or use alone.

HAND CREAM
Use when handling dry clay, to keep it moist.

MASKING TAPE
This is invaluable for keeping work in shape while it is drying.

MODELLING CLAY
There is a wide range of brands and qualities. Air-dried clay does not require firing, though you can strengthen some brands by baking or adding hardeners.

PAINT
Use acrylic artist's gouache for small projects, emulsion (latex) for large areas and for priming, and specialist paints for verdigris, crackle-glaze and metallic effects.

PAPER AND CARDBOARD
Use paper, tracing paper and cardboard for making templates. Tape clay to thick cardboard to dry flat.

PASTE FOOD COLOURING
Knead a small amount into clay. Concentrated ink or watercolour can also be used.

RELIEF OUTLINER
Apply straight from the tube to create embossing stamps.

SAND
Glue sand on to clay with PVA (white) glue for a textured effect.

TALCUM POWDER
Use on surfaces and cookie cutters to stop them sticking to the clay.

TILES
Embed pieces of broken tile in clay for a mosaic effect.

WIRE
Embed a wire hanging loop in the back of a piece. Use pliers to bend chicken wire to make an armature.

*Opposite: acrylic varnish (1); clay hardener (2); Dutch metal leaf (3); glue (4); hand cream (5); masking tape (6); modelling clay (7); paper and cardboard (8); paint (9); paste food colouring (10); relief outliner (11); sand (12); talcum powder (13); tiles (14); wire (15); wood glue (16); hooks (17).*

# EQUIPMENT

### CUTTERS AND MOULDS
Cake decorating suppliers are a good source of flower and leaf moulds. Cocktail sticks (toothpicks), drinking straws and fruit corers make neat indentations.

### HAMMER
Use a small lightweight hammer.

### KNIVES AND SCISSORS
Use the blade of a sharp knife for cutting clay and the flat side for smoothing edges. Use a round-ended table knife for indenting, a craft knife for cardboard templates and delicate areas of clay, and scissors for paper templates.

### MODELLING TOOLS
A wide variety are available, for shaping and smoothing clay. Use a balling tool to shape flower petals.

### PAINTBRUSHES
Build up a collection in different shapes and sizes. Keep separate brushes for glue and varnish.

### PENCIL
For tracing and marking designs.

### PLASTIC WRAP AND POLYTHENE (PLASTIC) BAGS
Cover spare clay with plastic wrap or store inside a polythene (plastic) bag to keep it moist. Moisten the inside of the bag if necessary.

### PLIERS AND WIRE CUTTERS
Use for forming armatures, bending and cutting wire for hooks.

### ROLLING GUIDES
Use two strips of wood of an even depth on each side of the clay. Use as a guide to roll the clay evenly.

### ROLLING PIN AND BOARD
Use a domestic rolling pin for large pieces of clay, and a small, cake decorator's rolling pin and non-stick board for small pieces.

### SANDPAPER, NAIL FILES AND EMERY BOARDS
Use to smooth rough edges on dry clay before sealing or painting.

### SAW
Use for cutting wood to size.

### SPONGE
Use a small natural sponge to apply paint for a mottled effect.

*Opposite: clay modelling tools (1); cutters and moulds (2); hammer (3); knives and scissors (4); paintbrushes (5); pencil (6); polythene (plastic) bags (7); pliers and wire cutters (8); rolling guides (9); rolling pins and board (10); sandpaper, emery board and nail files (11); saw (12); sponge (13); apple corer (14); nails (15); screwdriver (16); straw (17); cocktail sticks (toothpicks) (18); modelling knife (19); hessian (burlap) 20.*

# BASIC TECHNIQUES

*Modelling clay is an easy subject to master. Once you have grasped the basics, you will quickly produce projects that you can be quite proud of.*

MIXING CLAY WITH COLOUR

1 Use a concentrated colouring agent such as food colouring. Add gradually to achieve the shade required without making the clay too wet. The colour will dry a slightly different shade. Keep clay moist in polythene (plastic).

2 Roll the clay between your palms into a long sausage. Fold the ends to the middle and proceed to roll another sausage. Add more colour as necessary.

USING HAND CREAM TO KEEP CLAY MOIST

3 Repeat until all the colour is evenly distributed and you have achieved the desired shade.

Clay can dry out quickly, especially if the atmosphere is warm and dry. Always keep spare clay covered with plastic wrap or in a polythene (plastic) bag. It is useful to have some hand cream to mix into the clay to keep it moist. Do not add too much, as you do not want to make the clay unstable when dry.

## MIXING CLAY WITH HARDENER

1 Make an indentation in the clay and add some powder hardener following the manufacturer's instructions. If you are using a liquid hardener, dilute as appropriate first. Fold the clay over the powder and knead a little before rolling into a sausage.

2 Fold the sausage in half and add more powder hardener. Repeat until you have used all the powder you need.

3 Knead the clay thoroughly to blend the hardener evenly into the clay. This treatment makes the clay more difficult to work with, so keep it moist in a polythene (plastic) bag and use hand cream to soften it while working.

## USING ROLLING GUIDES

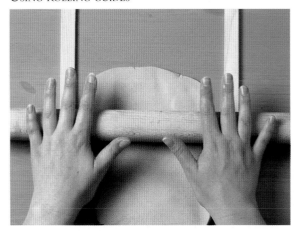

Rolling guides are lengths of wood or plastic of a set depth. Place the guides at each side of the modelling clay to be rolled out and roll out the clay until the rolling pin sits on the guides. This method ensures that the clay is the same depth throughout.

ROLLING OUT CLAY

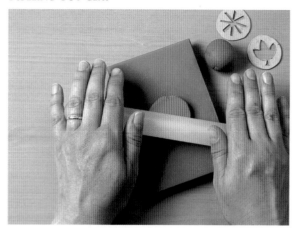

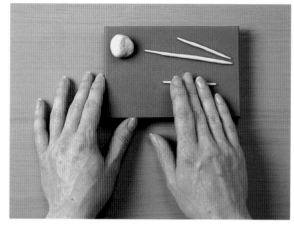

1 Work on a surface that can easily be wiped clean. A light dusting of talcum powder on the work surface and on the rolling pin helps prevent the clay from sticking. Take enough clay to complete the section you are working on. Flatten the clay with your hands then roll with the pin. Turn the clay around and keep rolling until you have a smooth, even slab.

2 A small non-stick rolling board and rolling pin designed for cake decorating are especially useful for rolling out small pieces of clay for delicate work.

CUTTING AROUND A TEMPLATE

1 Some brands of modelling clay can be quite fibrous when cut, so neaten the edges with a modelling tool or the edge of a knife as you work. Moisten the tool slightly with water as necessary.

2 Smooth the edges with a modelling tool for a more rounded edge or use your fingertips, lightly moistened with hand cream.

## EMBOSSING AND EMBEDDING

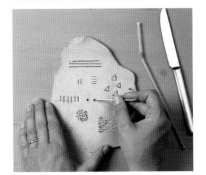

1 Before starting a project that requires surface decoration, practise on a spare piece of clay. Make small holes with a cocktail stick (toothpick), the rounded end of a knife, or by pressing a drinking straw into the clay and removing it with the plug of clay inside. Scratch the surface of the clay and emboss with found objects.

2 Press pieces of broken ceramic into the clay for mosaic work. Ease the surrounding clay gently around the sharp edge of the mosaic pieces to secure them.

3 Designs can be marked out on to the rolled clay by pricking with a needle or hatpin. Use tracing paper for the template, place it over the clay and prick out the design. Remove the template to reveal the design and work over the pinpricks with a knife.

## USING READY-MADE MOULDS

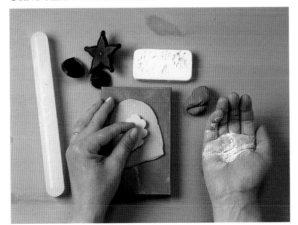

1 Give the mould a very light dusting of talcum powder to prevent it sticking to the clay.

2 Any excess talc can be removed with a water spray or a paintbrush dipped in water: don't make the clay too wet. Always clean the mould to remove particles of clay and dry thoroughly. Brush out any remaining pieces of clay with a bristle paintbrush.

## WORKING OVER AN ARMATURE

1 Very large pieces are made over a chicken wire armature. This will reduce the weight of the work. Allow the clay to dry slowly to prevent cracking on both the outside and inside of the armature. Make the armature from chicken wire, cutting and folding with pliers to mould into shape. Protect your hands with gloves.

2 Tear newspaper into strips and paint with diluted PVA (white) glue or wallpaper paste. Drape the strips over the armature to make a thin layer of papier-mâché. This stops the clay from protruding through the holes in the chicken wire as you mould the form.

3 Now start to build the shape with clay. Break off small pieces of clay and flatten them in your hands. Press the clay gently over the frame, smoothing the joins (seams) as you go and pressing the clay into shape.

## FILING ROUGH EDGES

## DRYING CLAY

When the work is dry, remove rough edges with a nail file or emery board. Sand carefully, as dry clay can be powdery and is delicate. Use a nail file for reaching small areas and fine sandpaper for large surfaces. Seal with PVA glue.

Dry clay slowly to avoid cracking. Cover with a damp cloth or plastic wrap to slow the drying process – especially work that has been made over an armature. Tape small, flat pieces to a firm background to prevent shapes curling, using a weight if necessary. Dry motifs for curved designs over a curved surface. Remove the tape carefully when the work is dry.

## REPAIRS

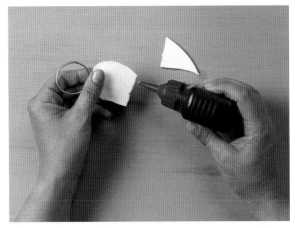

1 Cracks that form while the clay is drying can be repaired by adding a small amount of water to clay to form a thick paste. Press the paste into the crack and allow to dry. Repeat as necessary, then protect with a coat of PVA (white) glue.

2 Glue broken pieces together with strong wood glue, then protect with a coat of PVA glue.

## DECORATING

1 A variety of decorative techniques such as sponging and gilding can be used on modelling clay. Some types of self-hardening clay have a tendency to flake, so it is a good idea to seal the surface with one or two coats of PVA (white) glue first.

2 Apply paint with a paintbrush or sponge, dabbing the bristles into awkward areas. When the paint is dry, spray or paint with varnish to protect the work. Apply a minimum of two coats, but check the varnish on a small area first, as sometimes the colour alters slightly.

3 If you wish to add surface decoration, dampen the clay with water to help the decoration stick. When dry, check if any clay is loose and needs repairing. Apply matt varnish, to seal the surface and ensure that the relief work sticks to the base.

# TEMPLATES

*To enlarge the templates to the desired size, use a photocopier, or trace the design and draw a grid of evenly spaced squares over your tracing. Draw a larger grid on another piece of paper and copy the outline square by square. Draw over the lines to make sure they are continuous.*

SILVER-LEAF FINIALS, PP 34–7

VERDIGRIS CLOCK, PP 78–81

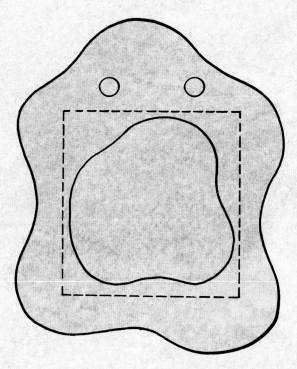

DECORATED FLOWERPOTS, PP 11–15

MOSAIC MIRROR, PP 48–51

BACCHUS GARDEN PLAQUE, PP 30–3

FLORENTINE BOXES, PP 60–3

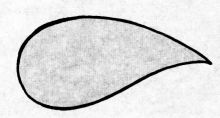

FLORAL LINEN SCENTERS, PP 45–7

FLEUR-DE-LYS WASTEBASKET, PP 74–7

LEAF WALL PLAQUES, PP 42–4

HEN MESSAGE BOARD, PP 24–6

ROCOCO WALL PLAQUE, PP 56–9

FLOWER GARDEN CHALK BOARD, PP 8–10

# SUPPLIERS

The specialist materials and equipment that you will require for the modelling clay projects featured in this book are available from any good art supply or cake decorating shop.

**Craft World**
Head Office
8 North Street
Guildford
Surrey GU1 4AF
*Craft superstores nationwide. All craft supplies including special paint effect kits, modelling clay, tools and equipment.*

**London Sugarart Centre**
12 Selkirk Road
London SW17 0ES
*Moulds and cutters for making flowers. Small rolling pins and mats. Will do mail order.*

**Alec Tiranti Ltd**
70 High Street
Theale
Reading
Berkshire RG7 5AR
*Modelling clay, modelling tools, gold and silver leaf.*

**Pearl Cake Decorating**
22nd Street
New York, NY 10001
USA

**Dock Blick**
PO Box 1267
Galesburg, IL 61402
USA

# ACKNOWLEDGEMENTS

The publishers would like to thank the following people for designing the projects in this book: Penny Boylan for the Decorated Flowerpots pp 11–15, Rose Drawer Handles pp 16–19, Gilded Curtain Tie-backs pp 20–3, Hen Message Board pp 24–6, Geometric Picture Frames pp 38–41, Leaf Wall Plaques pp 42–4, Floral Linen Scenters pp 45–7, Coil Pot pp 67–9 and Stone-effect Platters pp 70–3; Alison Jenkins for the Textured Lamp Base pp 52–5, Flower Garden Chalk Board pp 8–10, Summer Vase pp 27–9 and Silver-leaf Finials pp 34–7; Lucinda Ganderton for the Bacchus Garden Plaque pp 30–3, Mexican Candlesticks pp 64–6; Florentine Boxes pp 60–3; Fleur-de-lys Wastebasket pp 74–7 and Verdigris Clock pp 78–81; Cheryl Owen for the Mosaic Mirror pp 48–51 and Rococo Wall Plaque pp 56–9.

# INDEX